BLOODLUST

THE SEQUEL TO THE SUNDERLAND VAMPIRE

—

RICHARDVALANGA

Dedicated to

Anne Rice

"Go where the pain is"

Anne Rice's advice to me.

"I often think that the night is more alive and more richly coloured than the day."

- Vincent Van Gogh

ROLF

The red African sun looked like a gigantic fireball as it began to slowly set behind the mysterious blue island that shimmered in the orange glow that surrounded it. Heading through the calm golden sea towards this magical idyllic island was a large yacht called the Roker Seabird.

"What is it?" asked Alan Rolf, the owner of the Seabird.

Salty Laing, the boat's skipper, checked his computer charts.

"It's known as Vaaga, an island belonging to the Western Sahara I think, uninhabited according to what I have here; apparently it is under some sort of quarantine and has been for years, a delegated no-go area Alan."

"But it looks so beautiful" said Rolf's wife Cathy who had joined them on the bridge of their luxury yacht.

"Don't let the romantic view fool you Cathy, it must be off limits for a reason."

Cathy turned to Salty, "You mean disease, like a virus or something?"

"I guess so, there are other uninhabited islands in the area but none of them flag up dangerous like this one."

"Superstition?" thought Rolf out aloud.

"Possibly, these islands were once inhabited by roaming sea cannibals it was believed."

"Cannibals? Now that gives me the creeps" shuddered Cathy immediately as if some icy cold sea breeze had suddenly found her in the heat of the African evening.

Cathy's husband just laughed, "Ooh scary, maybe tonight we will be boarded by dead cannibal sea creatures, their faces covered in rotting bloody seaweed" and then he lunged at Cathy's neck like a vampire…

Cathy recoiled away from him.

"That's not funny Alan."

But even Salty began to laugh.

"Okay, we'll drop anchor here then" declared Rolf, "as near to that island as possible Salty."

"You want to take photographs of it, don't you?" said Cathy immediately because she knew her husband's obsession would not let a chance like this pass him by

"Yes… I do. The island intrigues me and why is it off limits, a beautiful looking paradise like that?"

"I would advise you not to go there Al… and anyway, you want to be back home Sunday night don't you?"

Rolf suddenly looked annoyed, "Yes… that meeting on Monday afternoon, damn it!"

"It's important then?"

"Yes, but…"

"But nothing Alan" interrupted is wife, "You have to attend it and you know it, we've had our holiday break and now it is time to get back to work."

"Slave driver" laughed Rolf as he opened one of the cool cans of beer that his wife had brought for them. He raised his can towards the island, "Until the next time mysterious island Vaaga, your secrets are safe for now."

Salty also opened his beer, the Seabird was now heading directly toward the island, "And I think it's just as well… something about that island gives me the jitters."

"Me too" added Cathy, "Look, I'm going to bed now, you two better not spend the night drinking; we have to up anchor at six in the morning."

"Aye aye captain" laughed Rolf, "Don't worry love, we can handle a couple of beers."

Like Salty, Rolf was in his mid-fifties but his wife Cathy was almost twenty years younger than him. Rolf and Salty had been in the navy together but Rolf's family were rich and upon leaving the navy he had inherited the family business and quickly made it even more successful than it was.

Early in the morning, just before dawn was about to break and while his wife was still asleep, Rolf dropped the Little Bird tender which was housed at the back of the yacht into the calm waters of the sea and headed immediately for the island known as Vaaga, with him was his state of the art digital camera. Photography was one of Rolf's favourite hobbies, he had built up quite a portfolio of work over the years and had exhibited locally and even nationally. Vaaga was simply an opportunity he could not resist.

Things would have been different if Rolf had put his business commitments first, "Business before pleasure" Cathy had always said and Rolf had always thought that Cathy was wise beyond her years, it was one of the things that had attracted him to her.

***

Rolf actually felt like a naughty boy as he dragged the Little Bird ashore and anchored it into the sand. Looking along the beach, Rolf noticed something that they had not seen in the dark of the night… scattered beams of decayed wood, black and burnt and tall ancient wooden poles that stretched from the sand into the sea. On closer inspection, Rolf realised that this was the skeletal remains of many jetty's that stretched further along the beach.

Rolf picked up one of the burnt wooden remains and it crumbled to dust slowly in his hand.

"This must have been a thriving area at one time" murmured Rolf to himself but the scattered ancient remains made him wonder, *Tribal war?* he thought to himself and it did seem a logical conclusion, *and where there are jetty's there are villages* he concluded.

Rolf took a few photographs of the beach, the sun had risen and was higher in the sky now he noticed and he smiled because he knew Cathy and Salty would now be awake and he could hear his angry wife scolding him.

"The bloody fool, he knows that we are pushing it to get home in time" Cathy growled as she looked toward the island of Vaaga.

Salty was looking through his binoculars, "That's Al for you, he's definitely there; I can see the Little Bird… but I don't see him?"

Rolf had now noticed openings in the trees that were obviously wide pathways once, the temptation was simply too hard to resist.

"That flaming camera of his, it will be the death of him" continued Cathy back on the yacht.

"Well, let's hope it is not today Cathy" laughed Salty looking along the island's beach, "It looks like Vaaga has been deserted for years so I don't think Alan has much to worry about."

"No savage man-eating cannibals then?"

"No, just a savage beer drinking photographer, that's all."

Cathy and Salty immediately burst out laughing together which eased the tension within Cathy, "And that beer drinking photographer is going to get the sharp end of my tongue when he returns."

"I think I'd rather risk the cannibals" laughed Salty and once again Cathy had to join in with him.

Alan Rolf did not return to the Roker Seabird until the afternoon.

There was something different about him.

Rolf had wisely brought a machete with him which he used to cut through certain parts of the jungle pathway He had researched the islands in the area during the night and he was satisfied that there were no animals that posed a threat to him, maybe just a wild pig or two; so he had decided that there was no need for any of the Seabird's guns, the only thing he had to beware of though, was indigenous poisonous snakes and spiders... he would not realise the real danger of Vaaga Island until it was staring him in the face.

Shortly after cutting through the wide overgrown pathway, Rolf became aware of a gruesome discovery, tall wooden poles or what was left of them were embedded in the ground and on top of them were the remains of ancient human skulls, mounted almost like macabre trophies... *or maybe they are a warning* Rolf thought suddenly. Rolf took photographs of the pole skulls then continued along the pathway, he sensed that he was close to some sort of a village dwelling.

Shortly the trees began to thin out and to his delight, Rolf's theory was proved right as the area became spacious and flat that was surrounded by the island hills. What Rolf was confronted with was the remains of some large habitat that had obviously deteriorated over the years. Some of the large huts that remained looked like they had been burnt and some had been naturally eroded by the forces of nature and time. This was a photographer's dream but as Rolf ventured further into the village, it became more like a nightmare. The area was littered with skeletons, both adult and infant as if some unknown disaster had suddenly befell them. It seemed to Rolf that some of them were running away from a rough edged blackened square building that was still standing intact as it was made of stone. Skull poles surrounded this large dark building, which looked like it had been initially crudely built and Rolf guessed that it was probably the village temple. Rolf felt suddenly sick as he imagined the horrors that had most likely taken place inside the dark temple. But he knew that he had to enter, photographs of this temple would probably be the most important he had ever taken.

There were no wooden doors to the temple, if there had been, they had long since eroded. There was light inside though as the sides of the temple had large square openings along the top of it's walls. Rolf was pleased about this because he had foolishly forgot to bring a hand torch.

Inside the temple there were no skeletons or skulls which sort of surprised Rolf, the whole room was dark and foreboding with a smell of smoke that somehow seemed ancient and alien and at the far end there was what seemed like a large oblong black stone slab that was obviously used as some sort of an altar and this altar seemed to be peppered with small greenish diamonds that formed abstract lines which seemed to sparkle and glow with a pulsating menace in what light there was.

Then Rolf squinted his eyes because in the shadows surrounding the altar, he thought that he saw a blackened figure... a human form lying on the altar.

Rolf began to tremble slightly with excitement, *How could that be?* Rolf thought *Surely the body would have deteriorated by now, surely it should be just bone?* The dark lifeless body became a magnet for Rolf's curiosity but he approached the altar cautiously, sweating profusely now because he had the feeling that there was something unnatural about this... *maybe it is some sort of a carving, the remains of some effigy that the cannibals had worshipped?*

The dark figure was hideous, there was no skin, just muscle and flesh covered in a green puss on which worms and large insects were feeding but as Rolf took a closer look; it seemed that the human form was consuming and absorbing that which crawled upon it.

Rolf was now standing directly beside the gruesome black and green figure and as the light of his camera flashed, the eyes of the burnt creature opened...

"Hal hadha 'ant lusifar... hal eudt li'iinha' eamalika?" ["Is that you Lucifer... have you come back to finish your work?]

Rolf froze then immediately stepped back in horror, "Wha... what are you... are you a... demon?" stuttered Rolf sounding like an actor from some old forgotten horror movie.

The horrific creature was now sitting up on the stone altar, the light from the square windows above lit up it's face making it look like some dark devil from Hell.

"'Ana la 'afham artijaf lughatik wahidatan... lakiniy sa'afealuha qrybaan." ["I do not understand your language trembling one... but I will soon.]

Rolf instinctively turned and began to run toward the doorway, his camera swinging from his neck like a loose anchor that was trying to slow him down.

With unnatural speed, the creature was upon Rolf, pinning him down like a heavy bird of prey. Rolf's head had hit the hard stone ground first causing an instant concussion and as he he fought to keep conscious, he felt his trousers and shorts being roughly pulled down.

"What..." was all that Rolf could utter as the black creature entered him from behind...

"'Ant mahzuz, lan yastaghriq hadha wqtan twylaan... lam yataghadhaa faj mundh fatratin." [You are fortunate, this will not take long... Vaag has not fed for an eon.]

The creature thrust hard into Rolf and as the room darkened around him, Rolf felt a warm pain as an ejaculated liquid filled him suddenly… a liquid that began to consume him from within.

The pain increased and surged throughout Rolf's body…

The last thing he felt was his bones dissolving

And the extended mouth of the creature

On his mouth

Sucking the green bodily liquid and his life from him.

When the dark figure had finished his meal he rolled off Rolf who was now just a thin layer of empty skin that was still shaking slightly on the cold stone ground.

The creature called Vaag had devoured Rolf's inner body completely and as he lay full and satisfied an amazing metamorphosis took place…

Lying next to the withered hideous skin of Rolf was… Rolf!

An exact naked replica

Who was smiling

As the thoughts and memories of Rolf surged through him…

"You have a boat… good, this unusual boat will take me from this deserted island."

Vaag, who sounded exactly like Rolf, quickly dressed in Rolf's clothes then headed to the beach, and he took the object called a camera with him even though he was still not sure what it's purpose was.

Vaag stood staring at Rolf's dingy for a moment and then he looked out to sea to the Roker Seabird. He knew that he was now about to be bombarded by the memories of Rolf, it always happened after 'the consuming' but this time he knew that it would be harder because there was a new world technology to master but the yacht that he was looking at now would be the ideal place for him to complete his transformation; a day or so would do it, all he had to do was feign an illness to those on board.

Vaag untethered the Little Bird dingy and after studying and starting the small engine, he headed for the Roker Seabird. Vaag could see that Rolf's wife Cathy was on the bow of the yacht waving to him, he knew that the temptation to consume her would be strong but not straight away, not until his thoughts and plans were clearer. Vaag lifted his hand and looked at it, it was a strange sensation having skin again, he waved slowly at Cathy; this friendly custom was something new to him. Vaag felt excited by the new life ahead of him, a feeling he had not experienced for a very long time.

Vincent Harper leaned back on his studio chair and admired the portrait painting that he had just completed. Harper smiled, he was really renowned as a portrait artist and his last exhibition had been of local landscapes which had been a great success gaining him much recognition throughout the country. Tyne Tees Television had wanted to do an interview with him but he had declined saying that he would do it at some future date. Vincent knew that psychologically he was not yet ready for such a thing even though his state of mind was now much better than it had been for a long time and he no longer had to consult with any doctor because of it. However, there was one abnormal thing that he still craved and desired... and that was to become a vampire like Doctor Charles Richarde and Ella Newman.

Doctor Richarde had been one of Vincent's consultants at the Hopewood Park Hospital in Ryhope, Sunderland and Ella Newman was his part-time assistant. As Vincent sat staring at his portrait of Ella, he reflected on the circumstances that had led to Richarde and Ella revealing themselves to him.

Vincent had unbelievably become entangled in a ghost story, there were no other words for it and this had resulted in serious consequences for his fragile sanity that was on the verge of collapsing completely. Richarde and Ella had come to Vincent's aid but it did mean that they had to reveal themselves to save not only him but the two spirits involved too. It had been a wonderful ending for all concerned, the demons that Vincent had wrestled with during that strange surreal time were exorcised and his full recuperation had been able to start. Of course coming to terms with the reality of what had happened had initially been challenging for Vincent but the only negative from his point of view ultimately was that he was no longer required to see Richarde or Ella on a professional basis.

The end of the ghost story had taken place at Whitby Abbey and this setting had compelled Vincent to paint portraits of the two spirits that he had encountered there. Vincent had been so pleased with the paintings that he painted a portrait of Doctor Richarde from memory. The painting that he was now looking at in his studio was of Ella Newman and as he looked at her flowing brown hair and magnetic matching eyes, he realised that he was indeed in love with her. Vincent wanted to be one with her and he knew that would mean that he would have to become a vampire.

But could he really do that, could he really become a creature of the night, a creature that fed on human blood? The answer was simple, he could because the power of love had consumed him completely. His most recent girlfriend Candice Raines had deserted him long ago during the darkest days of his mental trauma so now there was no one else, now there was only Ella… and now it was time for her to see her portrait. Vincent's hand trembled slightly as he reached for his phone…

ELLA

The sun had finally set over Charles Richarde's and Ella Newman's ancient mansion Moonlux Manor which was set in the countryside between the coastal villages of Ryhope and Seaham, close to the Hopewood Park mental health hospital where Richarde and sometimes Newman worked as occasional consultants.

Ella did not recognise the number on her mobile phone but she answered it…

"Hello?"

"Hi… is that… you Ella?" Vincent stuttered nervously.

Ella recognised the voice immediately.

"Vincent, is that you, how did you get my personal number?"

"Yes, it is me. It has been some time but I needed to speak with you… I was given your number by Charles when he first began to see me at Hopewood, he said that if I ever needed to speak to someone to phone him or you at any time."

"And do you need to speak with us, how are you feeling at the moment Vincent? We and the hospital thought that you had fully recovered?"

"Oh yes… I am much better now thanks to you and Charles. What I am phoning you about is a painting, well, two actually."

"Oh I see… Charles and I went to see your landscape exhibition and we were very impressed, we each bought a painting and I am looking at the one I bought of Ryhope Beach right now."

"You both bought a painting? I did not know, I have not got round to checking the buyers list yet."

"I would imagine that you sold all of the paintings?"

"Yes… I did… but since then I have been working on portraits."

"Really?"

"One of Charles and one of you are my most recent."

"Really, that is simply wonderful Vincent and I bet that they are really cool."

"Well, I am pleased with them, considering that they were painted from memory… so this is one of the reasons why I am phoning you, I would like to give them to you both."

Vincent's voice was tense now and Ella sensed this.

"One of the reasons, what is the other reason?" Ella had to ask.

"I… have to talk to you Ella… I have to know more about what you and Charles are."

"You do? And do you think that is wise… and also, just what do you think we are?"

"You… are… vampires!" Vincent replied and the words seemed to stamp out of his mouth.

There was a slight chuckle from Ella then she replied, "Yes… I suppose we are and I have to say that you have proven that we can trust you because you have not told anybody, have you?."

"Of course I have not told anyone and just who would believe me anyway, with my recent mental health history?"

"Quite so Vincent, quite so… look, I will come and see you and I will answer your questions, I do feel that you have a right to know now and I am sure that Charles will not object because it will help ease your mind I feel."

Vincent's heart suddenly began to beat like it was going to burst, not because Ella had said that she would answer his questions but because of the simple fact that he would be seeing her again.

"I will see you tomorrow Vincent if that is suitable for you? I really look forward to seeing you again and I am also now looking forward to seeing the two portraits."

"I… just hope that both of you like them."

"I am confident and quite sure that we will, I can be at your house at eleven in the morning if you want?"

"The morning? But shouldn't you…"

"Shouldn't I what, be sleeping in my coffin?"

Ella's laugh was almost sensual.

"I will see you tomorrow Vincent, you can even make me a cup of coffee."

"Coffee?"

Ella continued to laugh then the call ended.

***

Just before the eleven the next day, Vincent was nervous, he was slightly annoyed by this because he knew what Ella was and there was no way that she would ever think about harming him in any way.

At eleven precisely, the doorbell to his house Starry Night rang and when he opened the door, Ella was standing there looking stunning in a black leather motorbike style jacket with a white t-shirt which displayed The Rolling Stones famous lip logo. Her head was completely covered in a detachable black hood though and all Vincent could see was Ella's ruby red lips. Behind her on the drive was a silver BMW sports car with tinted black windows.

After Ella had stepped into Starry Night, she lowered her hood, Vincent was still looking at her car…

"You… came by car then?"

Ella laughed, "The sensible way to travel by day I think."

Vincent shut the door, "Oh… I see, I think?"

"Yes Vincent, I am sure that you do… now where are these lovely paintings you have for me?"

"In my garden studio, I have a pot of hot coffee waiting there for you too as you requested."

Ella chuckled to herself as Vincent led her to the back of his house, through the conservatory and into the garden to his art studio. As Ella crossed the garden, she covered her head with the hood then removed it again once inside Vincent's studio.

"How lovely… it is spacious and tidy, not really what I was expecting."

"It was cluttered but I sold all my landscapes. Please take a seat Ella."

Ella sat down at a small intimate table that was set against the wall to the left and on the table was a pot of coffee, the steam from it indicating that it was still hot and next to the pot was a small white jug of milk and a plate of enticing buttered scones.

Ella looked at the scones and remarked, "How thoughtful of you Vincent" as he poured them both a cup of coffee.

"I… didn't know if..."

"If I ate things like scones?" Ella remarked and she had to laugh which eased Vincent's nervousness then she explained, "The answer is that I do, I can eat any human food… but I do prefer and need blood."

This sent an instant chill through Vincent and he gulped as he poured milk into his coffee, "But I thought…"

"I think that you may have read too many 'vampire' stories or maybe you have seen too many Hollywood movies concerning us dear Vincent… and I think that I need to tell you a thing or two but not until we have enjoyed our coffee and you have shown me your paintings."

Vincent was exited by this, his hand trembled slightly as he held the small jug of milk.

"Milk Ella?"

"No thank you, I do prefer my coffee black."

As they enjoyed their 'elevenses' Ella asked Vincent how he was, she knew that what he had been through in Whitby was something that not many mortals had experienced. Vincent knew that Ella was checking out his state of mind and he was in fact thankful for it and told her that he was feeling really well, better than he had for a long long time. Ella was obviously pleased by this and this in turn pleased Vincent. After they had finished their coffee and scones Ella had to say, "Now then Vincent, I think it is time you showed me my lovely portrait."

Vincent's studio seemed much bigger once you were inside it and it was split in two, one half was recreational and the other half was a conservatory extension and that was where Vincent worked. Thick beams of sunlight were shining through the glass roof onto the work tables and easels. Opposite where Vincent and Ella were sitting there were large housing racks for paintings to dry. There was space for about twenty canvasses on the racks but only three were taken. Vincent went to the rack and pulled out the portrait of Ella.

Ella joined him and her face lit up when she looked at the painting, "Oh my, this is gorgeous Vincent!"

"You… like it then?"

"I really like it… I have only had my portrait painted once before and to think that you have done this purely from memory is magnificent."

Vincent was sure that there was tear in her eye and he let Ella absorb the painting for some time as they discussed his unique technique and original way of working. Then Vincent pushed the painting back into the rack and pulled out his portrait of the two spirits and his portrait of Richarde…

"Do you think that Charles will like this Ella?"

"He will be absolutely amazed Vincent, I am sure of it. This is contemporary compared his old portraits he commissioned years ago."

Ella pushed the painting of Richarde back into the rack then pulled out her portrait again and continued to smile. Vincent felt so pleased, it was obvious that Ella did really like her portrait, "Charles' painting is dry but your one is still wet, you can take both of them now though if you want, they will fit in the boot of your car."

"Thank you so much Vincent, you have made an old girl very happy."

"Old"

Ella kissed Vincent gently on his cheek, her lips were warm, moist and sensual and he was instantly aroused.

"I am old by your standards Vincent, very old in fact… and I think it is time to answer your questions, questions like how I am now here during the day."

"Yes, that would be one of them" Vincent interrupted, "I mean, I thought that sunlight would be harmful to you?"

"Not harmful Vincent, it's just that it… look, come with me."

Ella walked to the conservatory side of the studio and stepped into the bright sunlight.

Vincent gasped, Ella's face was now completely white, it was as if she had suddenly turned to marble and suddenly her eyes were red and not brown and for the first time Vincent noted Ella's small sharp canine teeth as she smiled at him. Ella's face looked like the face of a little girl who was about to reveal her most kept secret to her best friend.

"I can see that you are shocked Vincent, this is why Charles and I avoid the sun when in the company of mortals… feel my skin."

Vincent's trembling hand reached out and touched Ella's fingers…

"Your skin is like stone, as hard as marble..." he stuttered with disbelief.

"The white skin is protecting my blood from the rays of the sun, we can harden it whenever we like."

"So you really are not human then?" Vincent blurted out then he felt as if he had insulted Ella but she showed no sign that this was the case.

"Oh, I am human, I mean I was but Charles is from Terralux."

"Terralux?"

"Look Vincent, I can see that my hard white skin has shocked you, let us take a seat and I will explain things to you in comfort."

ELLA'S STORY

As Ella sat down, Vincent went to the corner of the studio, next to the drying racks where there was a sink, and a counter with kettle on it next to a tall thin cupboard. Ella noticed Vincent looking at the kettle then the cupboard.

"More coffee Vincent?" Ella asked.

Vincent opened the cupboard which was full of various bottles containing different types of alcoholic drinks and mixers, "I was thinking gin and tonics Ella, I have a feeling that I just might need something stronger than coffee."

"Gin and tonic would be perfect Vincent, a little early for me perhaps but I think it is the right choice."

After Vincent had poured out two large drinks for them both, he took them to the table and noticed that they had been joined by a visitor. A black one-eyed cat was rubbing himself against Ella's legs and purring softly.

"That's Killer and I can tell that he remembers you."

"The cat that was in the car at Whitby?"

"You knew that he was hiding there?"

"Of course, our hearing and sense of smell are... more acute I should say."

"Killer was a stray at Ryhope Cemetery, you can sort of say that we both helped each other out the night I found myself there... and he can be a sly old thing, he only reveals himself to people he trusts."

"Then we have a lot in common" smiled Ella who sipped her drink then continued...

"I shall begin in Ryhope then... it was the year 1722, I was fifteen years of age and I was working as a housemaid for a rich landowner called Hinks. Hinks was a nasty piece of work, obnoxious, twisted and cruel and yet he kept up his social standing by being a regular churchgoer; he professed to being a Christian but in reality there was nothing Christian about him at all.

Hink's wife had died in a so-called accident, her neck broken by a horse fall but most of his staff thought otherwise, that Hinks had broken her neck during one of his vile drunken moods then he had staged the riding accident. Nobody questioned his word, just as today, money was power then.

Hinks raped me when I was fifteen, not long after he had killed his wife. He had returned from one of his usual heavy drinking sessions at the Toll Bar tavern and I was preparing his supper on the table in the kitchen for him. Hinks always liked to return from the tavern to a hearty fire and a bottle of brandy with fresh bread, cold cuts of meat and pickles. He would eat his fill and then stagger like the drunken lout he was up to his bed, usually not rising in the morning until eleven pm.

That night all the staff had retired to their quarters in the out-houses. I was alone in the main house, I had been given too much work to do so I was late preparing Hinks' supper. I remember being nervous because I knew that he was due back at any time. Just as I finished adding more logs to the fire, Hinks burst in…

"Why are you still here girl?" he slavered at me with contempt.

"I… was just about to leave sir… your supper is ready… and… the fire stacked now…"

I was stuttering and shaking, I was well aware of his spontaneous vile temper, especially after he had been drinking. He staggered toward me and I saw that there was now a different look in his eyes, his anger had turned to drunken desire… he hit me hard on the side of my face and I fell to the floor. He then picked me up and threw me against the table…

"No… sir… please" I gasped but his hand had hold of the back of my head which he banged down hard on the kitchen table causing me to almost lose consciousness… I could feel my clothing being torn and pulled from me.

Then from behind he roughly entered me causing me extreme pain…

It felt like I was in a bad dream, the worst of nightmares and that time had somehow stopped and his hard thrusting seemed to go on forever but in reality my ordeal was over within minutes.

"That's what scullery maids are really for" he slobbered into my ear and he sounded like some sort of demon, like the Devil himself even and I staggered away from the table as soon as I could…

"Now get thee gone wench… so I can eat my supper in peace."

Tears filled my eyes, I could hardly see as I ran from the kitchen and all I could hear was Hinks' sick laughter as I pushed my way through the cold night air outside.

That night I wanted to leave that house of horror, I wanted to get as far away from that place as I could but the reality was that I had nowhere to go, both my parents had died, there was no other family, Hinks had given me a job and a place to live as a favour for the church and at the time I had been very grateful.

Hinks never touched me again and when I came into contact with him as I attended my duties within the house, he acted as if nothing had happened that night.

Two months later I knew that I was with child and I knew that I had to do something before it became common knowledge. I would probably lose my job, become a figure of disgrace for Hinks and the church. After nights of tortured thoughts I foolishly decided that I would tell Hinks, I thought that he might be sympathetic to my plight because he would finally have a child which was something he had always wanted, surely he would take care of us both? But my reasoning was out of complete desperation, I really should have known what Hinks' true reaction would have been.

Hinks had been drinking again in that Toll Bar, the tavern on the coastal road from Ryhope village to Sunderland town. Apparently, with his drunken friends, Hinks had been talking about "What chambermaids are really for" and then boasting quietly to his innermost cruel friends about what he had done because he knew that it was arousing them. I know this now because that night Charles Richarde had been seated in that tavern, enjoying a jug of ale while he smoked his pipe looking out towards the night sea. Charles however had been listening to Hinks' vile conversation with his preternatural hearing and luckily for me he had decided to follow Hinks home because he suspected that Hinks was in the mood for more cruelty.

As I had done many times before, I prepared Hinks' supper that night and had built up a roaring fire for him but instead of going to my room, I stayed in the kitchen… and waited. It seemed like an eternity and minute by minute my anxiety increased until I could stand it no more and decided that I could not go through with it.

Just as I opened the back door of the kitchen, Hinks stormed into the room from the house door. He was drunk as usual, maybe more so. At first he seemed surprised to see me then a vicious smile slowly formed on his wide mouth which made me feel instantly uneasy. When Hinks was sober, his appearance was not unfavourable, he was not a tall man but he was stocky and muscular, thick wavy black hair covered his head, arms and hands and his hooded eyes were sunken on his square face. But when he had been drinking, these strong features took on a grotesque appearance, especially by candlelight; it was almost a Doctor Jeykll and Mr. Hyde scenario… and this scared me.

"Well now maid, what have we here? Are you waiting in the kitchen… for your master's cock again?"

"No… no sir" I trembled and I closed the kitchen door, "I… need to tell you something."

I had to hold my hands because they were shaking so much now.

"You speak when I tell you to wench… maybe afterwards" he drooled drunkenly.

And then he came towards me, loosening his thick leather belt…

It was now or never for me.

"I am with child!" I blurted out, "Your… child" and then my voice was softer, like it had broken, I must have seemed like a small submissive animal to him suddenly.

Hinks immediately stopped, it was as if my words had acted like some magical shield stopping him in his tracks. His eyes seemed to roll in his head as he tried to take stock of what I had just said.

"My… child?" he stuttered almost gently and I had never heard him like that before.

"Yes master… that night when you…"

"You lie slut!" he suddenly boomed and I knew at once that I had miscalculated, I knew that I had to get away from him and as I turned, Hinks' heavy boot kicked me hard in the stomach and I fell to my knees in agony. On a shelf next to the back door was a large kitchen knife which Hinks grabbed and immediately he thrust it hard into my back… I called out in pain and as I looked up I thought I saw a face at one of the kitchen windows. Suddenly the back door sprang open and in came Charles Richarde…

"Wha… who the fuck are you?" stammered Hinks.

"Your executioner" were Charles' only words and he jumped at Hinks and snapped his neck like a twig. Hinks slumped to the floor, sunken eyes still open in disbelief. My head was on the cold floor and the light in the kitchen began to darken… I was dying.

Charles gently removed the knife from my back then cut the palm of his right hand and held it to my mouth.

"Drink girl, drink, it is your only chance."

His blood flowed into me, warm and soothing down my throat and I felt a strange sensation surge instantly through me, I was still in pain, still weak but somehow I knew that I was now not going to die. Charles tore open the back of my blouse and rubbed his bleeding hand over my deep wound.

"You will heal now girl… but you will never be the same again."

His words puzzled me as he lifted me up like I was a child's floppy rag doll. I felt that I needed to rest, to sleep and Charles took me to one of the spare rooms and as I slept he washed the kitchen floor so that there was no sign of my blood. He then released Hinks' horse and set it free and took Hinks' body and dumped it at the side of the road not far from the Toll Bar… it would appear to everyone that Hinks had died from a riding accident just like his wife.

When Charles returned my eyes were open, I was feeling stronger, Charles' blood was causing my body to change.

"Good girl" he said warmly, "Now you need to write a letter and leave it on the kitchen table."

"My name is Ella sir" I said weakly and still a little disorientated by what everything that had happened.

"Well young Ella, your letter needs to say that you have left immediately for a new position in London. You can write can't you?"

"Yes sir, the church taught me."

"Splendid… they will not bother about you then when they learn about what happened to Hinks."

"And what happened to him sir?" I asked innocently.

"He has fell off his horse, that man should really not drink so much."

Charles was right, nobody was that concerned about me after they had heard the news about Hinks' 'accident' and Hinks had no next of kin so his land was eventually put up for sale and bought by Charles. I stayed with him and we have lived there until this day."

Vincent Harper sat still in his studio, stunned by what he had just heard. He poured two large gins and gulped his drink down in one go… then he looked puzzled.

"You said that you were fifteen when you became a vampire… but you look older now?"

"Vampire is your word Vincent, we are not vampires and I will come to that now… you might need another drink because what you are are about to hear is not what you are expecting I suspect."

RICHARDE'S STORY

"Charles is not from this world, he is from another dimension, another reality, the world of The Luxar is known as Terralux, where magic and science are one. Charles' real name is Cha'ri which would translate as Charles Richarde I suppose. Certain Luxar have special 'gifts' and older Luxar have the ability to open inter-dimensional portals to other realms using the unique power of the Luxstone and the Malos are able to sense when a portal ripple is approaching. Luxars live for thousands of years but do age in appearance, that is why I look slightly older now.

"And who are the Malos?" Vincent had to interrupt.

"Yes… I get ahead of myself. The language of Terralux is very similar to Latin I guess - basically, The Luxar means The Light Ones and The Malos means The Dark Ones, the evil ones, the battle between good and evil exists in and across many realms.

On Terralux, only the blood of animals is drunk by The Luxar, the animals are not harmed or killed and their blood regenerates, I guess they are considered as blood donors not food."

"And you can eat human food too, you ate my scones?"

Ella laughed, "And very nice they were too Vincent, every now and then though I crave human food… a good curry, that sort of thing" and again Ella chuckled, "Charles can eat human food too but it is blood that our bodies need to survive."

"So you only drink from animals?"

"Of course, we are not Malos… Malos will drink Luxar blood, they kill Luxar and have crossed through the portal into this reality seeking human blood for years."

"And the Luxar sent people like Charles to protect us?" asked Vincent.

"Very perceptive Vincent, yes you are right, Charles was sent here at the start of the English civil war, he is the protector for the north of England and Scotland."

"So if any Malos appear and start killing humans then he…"

"He kills them or sends them back through an open portal to be captives of the Luxar Elders… The Luxar are a peaceful race but evil is evil and has to be dealt with severely. If the Malos were able to cross the portal to this realm in numbers then this reality would be in serious trouble."

"So Charles is a sort of policeman?"

Ella laughed again, "Yes, Vincent, I suppose he is."

"Does he not miss Terralux?"

"Yes, he told me that at first he did, then he grew to love this world and this country as he watched it develop and he has stayed as Protector ever since, at the moment he has no wish to return."

"Has he ever been back through the portal?"

"Yes he has, the Luxar Elders concerned with this area regularly need updates and he returns to discuss how things are here."

"I would love to go there" Vincent blurted out, "Have you ever been to Terralux?"

"No… I have not, not yet, when Charles goes there, I keep watch for him here… and also I think it would be very dangerous for you to even contemplate going there, even under the protection of The Luxar."

"Why is that?" Vincent asked rather naively.

"The obvious Vincent, you would be a delicacy and a target for The Malos that have infiltrated Luxar territory and they do abduct humans... enslave and breed them for food."

Vincent gulped hard and took another large drink of gin.

"So... so-called alien abductions maybe Malso abductions?"

"Yes I suppose so and as I have said Vincent, evil exists in most realities... and now I think I have told you all what you wanted to know."

Vincent reflected on all that he had just heard and it was totally unbelievable to him and yet the proof of it all was sitting right in front of him.

"It is incredible... and yes, not exactly what I was expecting and my stomach is turning now at the thought of those poor abducted human prisoners."

"The Luxar will try and save as many of those humans as possible which is very dangerous for the Luxar obviously; some will be sent back here after an amnesia treatment which will help them to forget, that is part of Charles' work at the hospital and at a place called The New Sanctuary, the rehabilitation of Malos abductees. You mentioned that it is not what you were expecting, so what did you expect Vincent?"

"Oh, I dunno... dungeons, coffins, crosses, maybe even a werewolf or two?"

And this time they both laughed.

"We'll leave all that to Hollywood shall we" said Ella with a broad smile on her face.

"Yes" replied Vincent, "But I have not changed my mind, in fact it has increased my desire."

"What desire?"

"To become a vampire... sorry, a Luxar."

The look on Ella's face turned suddenly stern, "That is something beyond me, something like that would be Charles' decision. Your life would never be the same... remember that your skin will become marble white, your eyes as red as blood when in daylight, you will shun the rays of the sun when with others... and what about your friends, your girlfriend?"

"I have no real friends now, no girlfriend, they all thought that I was mad, y'know, the mad artist."

"But your recent exhibition success, surely..."

"Oh yeah, I've had a few phone calls, congratulations but..."

"But what?"

"But... it is you that I need now, you I love."

Ella remained silent for a moment, stunned at this unexpected outburst by Vincent and he was sure that she was blushing. Ella took hold of his hand...

"Vincent… that is the nicest thing I have heard for a long time" and she kissed him gently on the cheek.

"Are… you and Charles, are you…" he stammered.

"Oh… no, Charles is like a father to me, he was my saviour and I will always love him for that."

"But he is not your lover?"

"No… I have never known real love as such" Ella replied and there was a great sadness to her voice.

Vincent looked directly into Ella's eyes but said nothing. Ella suddenly stood up.

"Look, I must be getting back now… and I can take your beautiful portraits?"

"Yes… yes, of course."

"And what are the prices?"

"Don't be silly Ella, all that I ask of you is that you tell Charles about my desire."

"Yes, alright I will do that" and once again she kissed Vincent on the cheek. Ella saw that killer the cat had jumped onto her seat and she was sure that Killer was sitting smiling as he purred with content.

CATHY

As soon as Vaag was on the Roker Seabird, he received a heavy scolding from Cathy Rolf at the rear of the yacht.

"And just where the Hell have you been? I suppose you decided that photographs were more important than the meeting?"

Vaag just stared at Rolf's wife, curious about the shapely creature in front of him who was talking just a little too fast for him to really comprehend what she was saying.

"Okay, cat got your tongue... or maybe it was those bloody cannibals? Got any photographs that will astound the world then?"

Vaag looked at the camera that he had strapped over his shoulder, he was not quite sure how it worked but he was certain that it was the contraption that the woman called Cathy was referring to.

"And look at the fucking state of you, go get a shower and change those stinking clothes, you look like you have been rolling in shit... I'll go and tell Salty to get us moving immediately, we might just make it back in time."

Cathy stormed off to the bridge and Vaag took stock of his surroundings... *shower, cabins below* he thought, then made his way below deck. Vaag showered thoroughly then went to bed immediately afterwards, he knew that sleep would speed up the memory process.

***

At eight in the evening Cathy went to wake her husband. When Vaag opened his eyes, Cathy recoiled back away from him, she was sure that his eyes were green.

"What... do you want?" was Vaag's blunt question, his English sounding broken and strange as if he was forcing himself to say the words.

"I want you to get up, you have been asleep since the afternoon for Christ's sake!"

"I am... not well... have... a fever."

Cathy put her hand on Vaag's forehead.

"You don't seem to be burning up?"

"I... feel sick."

"Well if you have contracted some exotic cannibal disease then it is your own fucking fault."

"Cannibal?"

"Yeah, y'know, those guys that cook people in pots then eat them, the ones you went looking for."

"I only… went to take photo… graphs."

"And now you're bloody sick… well I'm going to sleep in the spare cabin tonight, I don't want to get what you have got."

"It… would be wise… if you did" Vaag felt compelled to say which surprised Cathy Rolf as she was about to step through the cabin door.

"What?"

"Just… in case."

"Yeah… I don't want your fucking cannibal bug that's for sure. Sleep for the next couple of days if you want, we will be back home by then."

"Home?"

"Sunny fucking Sunderland my dear."

"I will look forward to… sunny fucking Sunderland."

Cathy looked at the pathetic looking pale creature lying on their bed, she sensed that there was something not right about her husband, she could tell, *maybe he is not trying to avoid the meeting, maybe he really is ill?* She just hoped that his sudden strange malady was not contagious.

***

Vaag remained in Rolf's cabin for three days, Cathy brought him his food which he pretended to eat and which he either flushed down the toilet or threw out of the cabin window.

Cathy became increasingly worried about her isolated husband. On the bridge of the yacht, Salty Laing asked her, "How is the patient then?"

"I just don't know Salty, I have only known him to be really sick just once or twice; he never even gets a cold usually."

"Must be just some sort of bug then, he'll be alright soon man."

Cathy did not reply.

"There is something else worrying you, isn't there?" Salty quickly added.

"It's… like it is not him, it is like he is someone else, I can't put my finger on it. All he does is lie in bed and look at his laptop, like he is studying something… and his skin, there seems to be no wrinkles and his his hair is suddenly jet black again, no grey hairs."

"Maybe this holiday has done him good then?" Laing replied half jokingly then, "Look, we have made up the lost time, in just one more day we'll be home, I reckon about midnight Sunday if the weather holds… if he is still not better by then then we will take him straight to a hospital okay? Why not tell him to get his cannibal island pictures ready for an exhibition, that will perk him up."

That night Cathy Rolf could not sleep, she could not get Rolf's camera and it's pictures out of her mind for some reason. Cathy's cabin was directly opposite her husbands and as quietly as she could she entered his cabin... her husband was sleeping, the laptop still open on his chest. She gently clicked the laptop back into life, strangely worried that she would wake her husband...

What Cathy saw astonished her, pages and pages of research about Lucifer the Fallen Angel, Lucifer the Devil and his kingdom of Hell.

My god, what the fuck is all this shit, has my husband suddenly become some sort of a Satan worshipper? What the fucking Hell happened on that island?

Cathy closed the laptop, grabbed Rolf's camera which was lying discarded on the floor next to the bed and quickly returned to her cabin. Immediately she accessed the camera's digital memory and was sickened by what she saw, especially the picture of the black figure on the stone altar...

At that precise moment, Vaag entered her cabin.

"Are you looking at something my dear wife, something you would rather not see?" he said rather sinisterly.

"I... was just curious Al... I just wanted to see what that island Vaaga was like, that is all."

Cathy's heart was beating fast, she was feeling anxious and scared by his presence and she had never ever felt this way with her husband, it was unusual to say the least and she knew it .

"My island... is beautiful, but it was definitely time to leave" saiid Vaag slowly.

"Your island... what the fuck are you talking about?"

"Hush now my sweet, you will waken Salty."

"I fucking hope I do because now you are freaking me out!"

"Then that is a shame because I wanted to spend more time with you, to learn from you and to fuck you."

"More time, fuck me? Just what do you mean Al?"

Suddenly Vaag sprung at Cathy and pinned her down onto the bed, holding her mouth tight so that she could not scream, his strength was much greater than that of her husband and this surprised Cathy. With his other hand, Vaag ripped Cathy's panties from her which were underneath the large t-shirt she had been sleeping in.

Cathy tried to call out but it was no use, Vaag's grip was vice-like. Vaag entered her but he was too large and this caused excruciating pain for Cathy...

Then the green acid began to flow from his penis...

"Do not fight it my love, I will be swift, tonight we will be one."

As it had done with her husband, the acid dissolved all of Cathy's internal organs, including her skeleton too.

Then Vaag's elongated mouth closed over Cathy's mouth and proceeded to drink from her at a unnatural rate.

Cathy's dead eyes stared in disbelief at the monster in front of her and were the last things to be sucked into Vaag's vile mouth, it was almost like the flames of two candles being extinguished.

Vaag brushed her hollow skin to the floor like the discarded skin of a fruit he had just devoured and then waited for the transformation to begin. Vaag knew that they were close to their destination and he now knew how to control the yacht. And in the morning he would have the human known as Salty Laing for breakfast then in the evening he would explore the land called Sunderland.

SALTY

Just before dawn, Vaag quietly entered Salty Laing's cabin. He did not wake Salty, he just caressed Salty's rough spiky beard with the fingers of Cathy. Vaag then lifted the single duvet and gently slid onto the bed beside Salty.

Vaag felt Salty harden in his sleep as the body of Cathy rubbed herself sensually against him. Softly she removed Salty's shorts, Vaag knew that Salty had been drinking heavily again because of the strong alcoholic aroma surrounding him, Salty did not waken.

Vaag guided Salty Laing's hard penis into the body of Cathy Rolf and began to slowly suck at him from within... a sudden sharp pain within his penis caused Salty to open his bloodshot eyes...

"Wha... what are you doing Cathy?"

"Ssh... relax, it will not take long" Vaag whispered.

"But what about Al... this is wrong!"

Salty tried to break free from Cathy but he was too late, Vaag's deadly green acid was now coursing through his body.

"My... God... the pain!" cried out Salty.

"Your God has deserted you, I'm afraid" commented Vaag with sarcasm.

"Wha... the fuck is happening?" Salty managed to ask as he felt his consciousness weaken and begin to fade.

"You are dying Salty but not for long."

"What... do you ... mean?" Salty whimpered and they were his last words as the inner protrusion from the mouth of Vaag closed upon Salty Laing's mouth. Within minutes, Vaag had satisfied his dark thirst again.

***

As Salty Laing, Vaag guided the Roker Seabird to it's destination on the North East coast of England. At eleven thirty pm, he moored the yacht at the Roker Marina in Sunderland and Vaag was pleased with his new sailing skills. Vaag was also interested in his new surroundings, the new star patterns in the sky, the cooler air, the different smells that came to him on the night breeze, the faint sound of moving traffic in the distance, even the gliding night birds and the sound of small animals scurrying under the cover of darkness intrigued him.

The boat was berthed next to a vessel of similar size called The Night Owl. Vaag watched from the bridge as a tall blonde haired woman on The Night Owl waved goodbye to two friends, she then turned toward the Roker Seabird and shouted, "Hey Salty... Salty, glad you're back... come aboard the Owl, we can have a late drink."

Vaag grinned and waved back to the desirable shapely woman.

"Yes, I would like a ... late drink."

EASTLEY

Vaag wasted no time in boarding The Night Owl and was greeted by the woman with the blonde hair who was holding two large drinks that were bubbling brightly in the light of the moon.

"Champagne, I thought Salty, welcome back… I didn't see Cathy and Al disembark though, how are they?"

"They are… fine" stuttered Vaag as he was suddenly filled with the confusing memories of his three victims combined.

"I'm sure they are, maybe they will join us soon?" replied Janet Eastley, "Let's sit up front on the bow and you can tell me all about the journey, if you are not too tired that is?"

Vaag's eyes seemed to sparkle in the moonlight.

"No, I am not tired."

"Well, you sound it but I am sure that the Champagne will perk you up."

"Yes, I am sure it will."

Eastley sat on the side seat on the right hand side of the yacht and looked up to the moon, she was a beautiful woman with a full figure who was in her late fifties but looked much younger.

"It's so quiet tonight, so peaceful, Sunday nights here usually are."

"That is good" said Vaag looking around the marina, it was as if they were the only two people there.

"It is good, sometimes those late night boat parties can get a bit annoying."

Vaag looked at Eastley as if he was studying her, "You live here, on this boat?"

"C'mon Salty, you know I live in Whitburn, but I do like to come here as much as I can."

Eastley looked back at Salty, there was something different about him but she was not sure what, his voice or maybe the way he talked was not right *but then maybe he is just a little exhausted from the long journey back to Sunderland* she thought. Eastley poured out more Champagne for them both.

At about two o'clock in the morning, slow drifting clouds had obscured the light of the moon and it was Eastley who was now the one that was tired and more than a little bit drunk.

"Well Salty, if I am bushed then surely you must be?"

Salty's head seemed to turn a full 180 degrees as he quickly scanned the marina then his hand clamped hard onto the mouth of Eastley…she stood up and tried to scream but it was no use. With his his right hand Vaag unzipped his trousers then ripped Eastley's tight shorts from her, Eastley was now in a drunken daze, completely in shock by what was happening. Vaag violently entered her, ejaculating his green acid at once.

Eastley tried to fight back but the acid took effect immediately, her hand gripped the handrail above her seat and she leaned backwards as Vaag's long mouth closed over her mouth… and he began to suck the life from her. Within minutes it was over and Vaag was full and satisfied again. Eastley's withered skin and what was left of her body slipped over the handrail and dropped into the water like the remains of a discarded deflated inflatable doll.

Vaag watched with curiosity as the now gruesome face of Eastley sunk below the waterline then drifted away with the slow undercurrent. The moon had reappeared from behind the rolling night clouds and Vaag looked at his new face in the still waters that were now acting like a dark ghostly mirror…

"She is quite beautiful… and rich too, her residence will be the perfect place to reside while I explore this new world."

Surprisingly though, Vaag was now tired, he had been affected by the Champagne, his body did not need human food or drink but sometimes he did like to indulge himself and he had enjoyed the various wines and intoxicating drinks that his subjects had brought him on his island of Vaaga.

But that was another world, another time thought Vaag, t*he days before Lucifer* he remembered and suddenly the old anger surfaced within him but he did not want to dwell on it, he decided that he would sleep then come the morning light he would find the home of Eastley in the place called Whitburn.

BULMER

Detective Inspector William Bulmer was a hardened policeman, a man who only had a few months left in the police force until his retirement. Bulmer was known as 'Bull' in the police department because of his unshaven rough appearance and personality. Bulmer had the misfortune of always getting the hardest assignments, something he sort of took as a compliment and something he had grown accustomed to over the years. Bulmer had assumed that he had seen it all but standing in the cabin of Cathy Rolf changed this thought immediately.

"Have you ever seen anything like it Bull?" asked his astonished assistant Davis. Bulmer did not answer straight away, he just stared at Cathy Rolf's withered flat skin in the floor, her crumpled t-shirt making it look even more macabre.

"No Bob, I haven't, for a moment I thought that we were on the set of some horror movie, or maybe a fucking sci-fi?"

"We're in the Twilight Zone alright Bull, what the fuck could have done a thing like that?"

Bulmer laughed but it was an unsympathetic hollow laugh, "The only thing I can think of is a fucking vampire... but the bones, the internal organs, all gone like they never existed and no trace of blood anywhere. Has anybody from forensics looked at this yet or the other one?"

"No Bull, they wanted to wait for you."

"What, like I'm some expert on missing bodies without their skin...maybe it's fucking aliens for Christsakes?"

Davis looked at Bulmer then he asked, "And what about the missing guy Rolf who owns this yacht, do you think he's the murderer?"

"Don't know, he has to be the prime suspect but I think he's probably another victim, we still need to look for him though. We'd better tell forensics to get these skins bagged and taken away immediately."

"Immediately, don't you want to check the rest of the boat out?"

"Not yet Bob, that poor woman might have died from some bacterial parasite, this boat needs to be isolated."

"Fucking Hell Bull, do you mean like an alien virus?"

Davis looked worried and stepped back away from Cathy Rolf's skin.

"I mean like something unnatural has happened here... what we need to do is check the marina cctv."

Bulmer and Davis accessed the marina cctv back at police headquarters back in the centre of Sunderland. There was only one camera along that part of the marina and it showed the jetty walkway and the back of the boats. The Roker Seabird was moored in the number 1 spot reserved for it and number 2 was Eastley's yacht.

Davis scrolled through the time log until he came to Sunday night and when the Roker Seabird had docked there. Bulmer and Davis now had all the details of who was on the yacht and the journey log.

"That must be the guy called Salty Laing" Davis said looking at the black and white image of Vaag on the Seabird then they saw Eastley saying goodbye to her friends and then turning toward Vaag. As Vaag stepped onto Eastley's yacht, Bulmer said to Davis, "Okay, we have to find out who that woman is, she has to be the last person who saw Laing alive… scroll on."

Davis continued through the timeline but Salty Laing did not reappear, only Eastley, who then walked away down the jetty walkway then she turned right to go to the marina car-park.

"It doesn't make sense Bull" said Davis, this guy Salty does not leave Eastley's yacht… how did his skin… get back on his yacht?"

"I don't know Bob, all I know is that we have to speak to that woman, it's been two days now since that night; we don't want any possible leads to go cold."

After checking with the Roker Marina authority, the two detectives found out the details of who the woman was and where she lived in Whitburn.

"Right Bob, let's go and see this Janet Eastley."

"You don't really think that she is capable of such a thing do you Bull?"

"Who knows Bob… y'know, I'm thinking some sort of acid here, it's like there bodies were injected with something like that; isn't there a spider that sprays acids onto it's prey?"

"Don't know Bull but what sort of acid would not dissolve the skin too?"

"Hell, I don't know man, we'll leave that one for our forensic science guys."

"But surely she would need a special place for something like that… a metal bath, a bloody laboratory for Christsakes… how could it have been done on a yacht that had just returned from a long sea voyage Bull?"

"Like I said, I'm still not sure how it was done in the first place… look, we need to talk to Eastley before it hits the news."

"You know it's too late for that Bull, that part of the jetty is cordoned off now, the local news teams will soon be aware of that."

"Shite… and they'll be wondering about the Contamination Unit too."

"It's gonna get out Bull, sooner or later, the female victim was a well known business woman like her missing husband who has to be some sort of a suspect, doesn't he?"

"Yeah, where is he I wonder and was he still on the yacht even though there is no footage of him leaving it? Damn, this is some bloody weird conundrum Bob, we have a missing guy and two gruesome human body skins like nothing I have ever seen or heard of before… c'mon, let's go to Whitburn then and speak to Eastley about the mystery of the guy known as Salty and why there is no cctv footage of him leaving her yacht."

EASTLEY

After finding Janet Eastley's car in the adjacent marina car-park and accessing her memories, Vaag had eventually managed to control the strange metal vehicle with the four wheels. Driving slowly away from the marina, Vaag became increasingly more confident in controlling Eastley's Mercedes and by the time he arrived at her cliff-side residence he was thoroughly enjoying the experience. The house of Eastley was large and was one of the two last residences on a road called Cliffhouse Drive and opposite her home, Vaag could see the top of a very stylish white art decor building in the distance. Behind Eastley's house were the cliffs and the great expanse of the North Sea.

Vaag spent the morning familiarising himself with Eastley's luxurious abode then on the afternoon he took a refreshing walk along the cliff edge. *This land is not as warm as I would have liked but I will grow accustomed to it* thought Vaag and then he looked out at the sea below and thought about his island Vaaga that he had left behind.

Vaag had been a god there.

A God of Cannibals.

A god that travelled the world over the years in the sturdy boats that his people had made, in search of someone similar to him, a shape-shifter that devoured the innards of humans.

Vaag was in fact looking for a companion he would not want to eat…

But his search was always fruitless.

So he always returned to Vaaga.

The place where he had come into being.

The place where his body and consciousness had evolved over thousands of years.

And he loved his island…

He loved the taste of his people.

A people who had become cannibals because of him.

The people known as the Vaagen, who were feared throughout the world in their day.

Could that be achieved here, in this new age?

Probably not, the world had developed so much and these new technologies excited Vaag. There was so much to be explored again and his search for a companion would continue.

Vaag sniffed at the fresh sea air breezing across his face, *there are new people to be devoured here, new smells, new tastes, new sexuality...*

Vaag was alive again.

And if Lucifer comes again, I will devour him!

***

After his cliff-side walk, Vaag took Eastley's Mercedes and drove through all the near cities, Newcastle, Sunderland and Durham and on the evening he returned and opened up one of Eastley's many fine wines and sat in her lush rear garden. It would be a very long time before he needed an acid feast again so there was no hurry to feed. Vaag decided that in the morning he would check out all of Eastley's friends on the phone communicator and in her diary and start thinking about who his eventual next meal will be. This would be something he knew he would enjoy, he always liked to play with his food before he ate it.

BULMER

The journey to Whiburn by car was not far and as Bulmer started up his battered Ford Escort, Davis had to comment, "When are you going to get rid of this old relic Bull?"

Bulmer glared at Davis with his stony blue eyes.

"I'm thinking of getting a new one when I retire but this is my baby, we retire together."

Davis smiled as Bulmer lit up the cigarette that had been nestling behind his ear.

"And I suppose you're going to give up smoking too when you retire?" Davis said as he opened his car window slightly to let the unwanted smoke out.

"Aye, that's right, I've got my retirement all planned."

Davis smiled again because he knew that Bulmer was *talking out of his arse, Bull has nothing planned.*

"It's going to be sun, sand and sex Bob, with plenty of beer to wash it all down."

"You'll be telling me that you are going to marry your long suffering Susie next."

"Aye, I might even do that too, if she's lucky."

Bulmer's raucous laugh was harsh sounding and infectious and Bob smiled again as he shook his head.

Soon the pair of detectives were driving through the small coastal area of Seaburn when Davis suddenly thought…

"Hey Bull, I think that there may have been something that we have overlooked."

"Oh yeah Tonto, and what is that then?"

"This Eastley that we are going to see… if it is some sort of parasitic virus then won't she be infected?"

Bulmer stopped the car suddenly beside the recreational area known as The Stacks. Bulmer thought for a moment then replied, "We've been on the boat Bob, if it is contagious then there is a chance that we have got it already."

Davis gulped hard, he did not like the idea of becoming a withered empty skin, "So that means we could infect her, doesn't it?"

"The man called Salty has been on her boat remember... look, we're over-thinking this Bob" said Bulmer as he picked up his phone.

"Who are you calling Bull?"

"Forensics."

After a short discussion Bulmer ended the call...

"And?"

"Early days but they haven't found any sort of parasitic virus as yet Bob, so that means we're probably in the clear for now."

"What do you mean for now?"

"They have found traces of an acidic substance but they don't know what it is yet, chances are it is not infectious they say."

"How come you never get a straight answer from those science bods?"

"I've had years of it, they can drive you fucking nuts if you let them... right, let's go to work."

Within minutes they were parked outside of Eastley's residence. As he looked at the tall metal silver security gates Davis had to remark, "She must have some fucking money Bull?"

"Aye, her yacht The Night Owl was just as big as Rolf's Seabird."

Davis stepped out of the Ford Escort and went to the intercom on the wall beside the gates.

It was now late afternoon, a hot day at the start of June and Vaag had been sitting in the garden going through Eastley's diary. He was in the kitchen making himself a tall cool cocktail when he heard the sound of the intercom. At first he did not know what the sound was then he saw the green flashing light on the small white box on the wall beside the door. There were four buttons below the small light, one said SPEAK, one said OPEN, the third said CLOSE and the fourth said ALARM. Vaag pressed SPEAK.

At the main gate, the light for SPEAK flashed on.

"Hello, this is Inspector Davis, I would like with Miss Eastley if possible please."

"Inspector of what?" was Vaag's unusual reply.

"I'm from the Sunderland police department, am I speaking to Janet Eastley?"

"I am... Eastley, police are protectors who enforce the law are they not?"

This reply by Vaag puzzled Davis, her words were strange to say the least.

"Er... yes, that is what we do. We would like to speak with you about an incident at the Roker Marina on Sunday night if that is possible?"

Vaag was intrigued, he had not spoken with anybody in the flesh as Eastley yet, he thought that it would be interesting with speak to these 'policemen' and to find out what they wanted to know. Vaag pressed

OPEN on the intercom panel then went to the front door. Davis returned to the car and Bulmer asked, "We got the green light then Bob?"

"Yeah, but…"

"But what?"

"I dunno, she sounds kind of… weird."

"People with money always do Bob, they have different priorities to us peasants. C'mon, let's see if she knows anything."

Within minutes they were standing in front of Vaag.

"Come in policemen, we can sit in the rear garden and have refreshing drinks in the warm sun."

Warm sun? It's bloody roasting today thought Bulmer instantly as he looked admiringly at the shapely body of Eastley who was wearing a tight fitting miniskirt and a very revealing red bikini top. Bulmer and Davis looked at each other then followed Vaag to the garden and for some reason Bulmer felt like he was suddenly some sort of a servant.

"Please sit here policemen, I will bring a tray of cold drinks."

Once again Bulmer and Davis looked at each other, it was the way Eastly said policemen that was bothering them.

After Vaag had returned with the large gin and tonics he sat opposite the two detectives, he was now wearing large sunglasses. As Eastley, Vaag crossed her legs seductively and noticed that Bulmer was looking at her quite intently now. Vaag knew that Bulmer was interested in Eastley's body.

"Now, you have come to… my house, how can I help you?"

Davis spoke first which seemed to surprise Bulmer.

"Like I mentioned on the intercom Miss Eastley, it is about the Roker Marina, last Sunday night…"

Bulmer then intervened and got straight to the point, "I am Detective Inspector Bulmer Miss Eastley and it concerns a man known as Salty, we believe that you were the last person to speak with him."

"Why would you believe that?"

"The marina cctv Miss Eastley, we have seen footage of Salty getting on your yacht."

"Cctv?"

"Camera footage" replied Davis but he could not believe that he was having to explain what cctv was.

"Ah, cameras, moving pictures, I see."

Bulmer and Davis looked at each other again, both puzzled by Vaag's words.

"Yes, the man known as Salty did come aboard The Midnight Owl… we had late drinks under the moonlight then…"

"Then what?" interrupted Bulmer quite harshly.

Vaag looked intently at Bulmer before replying, Vaag liked this human called Bulmer, he seemed to have a strong personality and looked strong physically, *he would make a perfect meal* Vaag thought, then he thought about his reply… "Then he decided to stay the night on the boat."

"You slept together then?" Bulmer had to ask.

"That is quite a personal question Inspector, do you want to know the exact details?"

Vaag uncrossed Eastley's shapely legs and spread them so that Bulmer could see her black panties. Bulmer actually began to blush which was unusual for him and Vaag smiled seductively as Eastley, he did not think that Bulmer was someone who would be embarrassed by anything.

"I was just…" stuttered Bulmer, "trying to establish…"

"The exact details" interrupted Vaag, "are that we both slept in separate cabins unfortunately there was no sex between us. Salty said something about going for an early morning swim… and I never saw him again after that. Why do you want to speak to him Inspector Bulmer? I do hope that nothing terrible has happened to Salty, he was a really nice person" said Vaag but what he really meant was that Salty was really delicious.

The detectives glanced at each other, the press had not released anything about the marina incident yet at the request of the police because of the contamination aspect but Bulmer knew that the disappearance of the two Rolfs and Salty Laing would soon be big news. Bulmer decided that he had heard enough.

"Do you want another drink policemen?"

Bulmer was really tempted by Eastley's offer, he felt that he could interview this woman for hours in this setting with her dressed like that.

"Er, no thanks Miss Eastley, we really should be going now" Bulmer reluctantly replied.

Bulmer and Davis stood up and Bulmer shook Vaag's hand and was astounded by how hard Eastley's grip was.

***

Back in the car, Bulmer had to ask, "What the fuck did you make of Eastley Bob?"

"Bloody gorgeous, and I saw you looking between her legs."

"Yeah, and you too… never mind the Basic Instinct moment, I meant how she spoke."

"What like?"

"Like the way she called us policemen, like it was a new word or something."

"And she didn't seem to know what cctv was" replied Davis, "Maybe she has some sort of mental problem, she is getting on a bit."

"She's about my fucking age Bob but I have to admit that she doesn't look like it." Bulmer thought for a moment then added, "I think she knows something Bob and didn't you think it was strange that she knew what a camera was but not cctv? C'mon Tonto, we need to take a better look on that yacht now, now that we know that we are not going to be eaten away like some fucking baked potato."

RICHARDE

On the Sunday that the Roker Seabird was approaching Sunderland, Vincent Harper received a phone call from Charles Richarde.

"Hello there Vincent, I hope that you are well. It has been a long time since I last spoke to you and that is a good thing is it not?"

Vincent laughed as he knew exactly what Doctor Richarde meant.

"Yes, I suppose it is… but it was great to speak to and see Ella again."

"Yes, that is one of the reasons why I have phoned you. I would like to thank you for my marvellous portrait and to congratulate you on the success of your recent art exhibition.

"Thank you Charles, that exhibition made me focus again, helped me get my life back on track."

"I am sure that it did, you can see it in your paintings."

Richarde paused for a moment then continued, "The other reason that I am speaking to you is that Ella and I would like to invite you here to Moonlux Manor this evening for dinner, as an appreciation and thank you for your the portraits."

"Wow, Moonlux Manor, that sounds cool."

"Nothing formal Vincent, certainly not black tie and tails, you can come as informal as you like. Ella has said that she would love to cook for you."

"Ella is wonderful and I bet she is a great cook, I am so pleased that you saved her life."

Richarde became thoughtful, "Yes, I know that she has told you about her background as a kitchen maid… not many people know of this, only a select few."

"And me…"

"Yes Vincent, and you… the ghost story you became entangled with prompted this as we both know and I am glad and I should tell you that I think Ella is more than pleased."

This made Vincent's heart thump faster, *is Richarde trying to tell me something?* he pondered then the doctor continued, "So shall we say dinner at eight? Do not worry about transport as Ella said that she will pick you up at seven."

"I will be honoured to attend Charles and I am really looking forward to seeing you again."

Vincent's heart was still beating fast after the phone call had ended, what Richarde had said about Ella had really fired him up, he just hoped that he was not just imagining it.

MOONLUX MANOR

At seven pm exactly, Ella Newman arrived at Vincent Harper's house Starry Night. She did not get out of her car, she sat patiently and waited for Vincent. Within minutes Vincent was sitting beside her. He was dressed casually in black jeans, smart shoes and a short sleeved open white shirt. Ella was dressed in an expensive thin black dress which was almost a miniskirt which had a small embossed bat shape pattern which was not noticeable at first glance. She was wearing a thick white bracelet which was not ivory and around her neck was a white cross, this reminded Vincent that Ella was a Luxar and not a Hammer Horror vampire, still a blood drinker though and Vincent could not help feeling a little apprehensive by this still.

"You look absolutely stunning" said Vincent as Ella drove the car away from Starry Night.

"You look and smell good too Vincent, what is that aftershave?"

"A new one I found called Route 66."

"Get your kicks on Route 66 eh?" smiled Ella.

"I hope so" Vincent replied and Ella laughed as she turned the car cd player on.

"I hope you like Black Sabbath Vincent?"

"Oh yeah, Ozzy's Osbourne's Sabbath."

And Sabbath Bloody Sabbath blasted throughout the BMW.

"Well it is Sunday" joked Ella as they drove through the countryside lanes towards Richarde's Moonlux Manor which was not far from Vincent's house. Who Are You was playing when Ella stopped the car outside the large double doors to Moonlux.

"Wow, how old is that house, it looks more like a castle to me?"

"Yes, it was a small castle of sorts originally but obviously it has evolved over the years. It was built in the 1500's."

Once inside Moonlux Manor, Vincent was impressed, it seemed to be a mixture of the old and the new, the modern aspect of the decor was Ella's doing and Vincent realised this immediately.

"I recognise your input here Ella" Vincent said and she knew exactly what he meant.

"Well I do get away with things but Charles really is nostalgic for the past, he will never change, sometimes I think he preferred those times."

"I think it is a great balance, there is a great warmth to this place."

"Thank you Vincent, this way please" Ella said and she led him into a large dining room which was lit by candlelight and corner wall lights. Charles Richarde was waiting beside a large fireplace. A fire was burning but only a token fire. Richarde rounded the dinner table and went straight to Vincent to shake his hand. Richarde was more formally dressed with a brown patterned waistcoat and a red and white spotted tie. Vincent remembered how he always thought that Richarde reminded him of the Marvel comics movie character Doctor Strange.

"Vincent my friend, it is good to see you again. Dinner is ready to eat but first one or two aperitifs I think, please sit."

The dining table was not large, just right for about six people. Richarde and Vincent sat at opposite ends with Ella in the middle with the table for the hot trays and the drinks trays behind her.

"Champagne Vincent?" Ella asked popping the cork and then pouring out three glassfuls.

"Yes, thanks" Vincent replied and as he sat down at the table he surveyed the room. Four of his oil paintings adorned the walls, his portraits of Richarde and Ella were on opposing walls and next to them were the landscape paintings from his exhibition that Richarde and Ella had both bought.

Richarde noticed that Vincent looking at his paintings, "We may have to name this room the Vincent Harper room" laughed Richarde.

A very good idea Charles" added Ella and then raised her glass, "Here's to greater success for you in the art world Vincent" she said and Vincent looked instantly embarrassed but sipped his Champagne in appreciation of Ella's kind words.

"I think a toast to you two would be more appropriate" Vincent suddenly said.

"And why is that Vincent?" asked a puzzled looking Richarde.

"The work you both do that goes unnoticed."

"Ah, you refer to the threat of The Malos do you not? I know that Ella has revealed our background to you."

"Yes, the Malos that come through the portal from your world of Terralux to terrorise us."

"There has not been a portal breech for some time Vincent, thank God" said Richarde and he sounded pleased and grateful.

"God... you believe in God Charles?" asked a surprised Vincent. Richarde smiled...

"I believe in a greater entity Vincent, a Clear Conscious you might say...."

"So you believe in Jesus and angels... and the Devil?"

"Yes, I know that angels walk among us… and the real Devil is the Dark Conscious, the unseen evil force that can infest and effect us all in every realm and reality."

Vincent gulped on his Champagne but then wondered why he had reacted so, he had seen spirits, he now knew that 'vampires' were real, so why did the thought of angels actually existing surprise him? Vincent however had a more urgent thought than one of metaphysical realities, he was going to wait until after dinner before bringing up his desire but he could not resist the urge to mention it now.

"You know so much Charles, that is why I want to become a Luxar like you… I could help you fight The Malos."

Charles looked at Ella then smiled warmly, "Ella has told me about this Vincent but it is something my elders do not encourage."

"But… you transformed Ella into a Luxar?"

"That was to save her life Vincent, it was not planned, I acted on instinct and with compassion and this was explained as such to my Elders."

"So why can you not do the same for me?"

"The answer is simple Vincent, you may become Malos, you may turn evil and become a threat, one which I would have to delete from this existence."

"What, turn evil, why would I do that, you have been my doctor for some time, surely you know that I am not like that by now?"

"Who knows what may happen, the Dark Conscious may effect anybody at any time, even myself and Ella could succumb to it's evil touch."

"Surely not Charles?"

Richarde laughed, "I sincerely hope not but I hope you take my point, we simply do not know what the future has in store for us."

"We do not but none of us do, even your Elders I am sure…so there is no hope of me becoming a vampire then?"

Ella laughed, "You mean a Luxar Vincent."

"Sorry, yes I mean a Luxar."

"There is always hope for anything Vincent. Remember when you first came to me as a patient, you had all but given up completely but look at you now, how your work thrives" said Richarde looking again and pointing at Vincent's paintings hanging in the room.

Vincent was obviously disappointed by what Richarde had said and Ella knew this.

"Right you two, we can maybe discuss this later but now I am ravishing. I have cooked roast beef Vincent, I do hope that you like it rare?"

"Yes… yes of course we should eat, I am sorry for sounding so selfish."

"You are not selfish" said Ella as she served out the food, "I was human once too remember, I really understand how you feel Vincent."

Ella then went to the cd player in the corner of the room.

"A little ambient music while we eat I think, Brian Eno's Lux album is very appropriate don't you think?"

And as the beautiful music wafted through the dining room, the three friends tucked into their delicious meal.

***

After dinner, Ella poured out a selection of cocktails and the subject of Vincent's desire was never mentioned again. At one o'clock in the morning Vincent thought that maybe it was time for him to return home and at that moment Richarde's mobile phone rang, the call was from Hopewood Park hospital.

"I am afraid there is something of an emergency, a patient of mine, I am sorry but I must go."

"Yes, it is late now Charles, I was thinking that I should get back now; I will phone a taxi."

"I will take you home Vincent" said Ella.

"But you have been drinking?"

"Not as much as you two, come we will go now."

Vincent shook Richarde's hand and thanked both him and Ella for a superb evening then at the front door in front of Ella's car he said to her, "It has been a great night Ella, I have really enjoyed it."

The bright moonlight was shining directly into Ella's eyes making them the most beautiful things that Vincent had ever seen.

"The night does not have to end Vincent… and you were right, I have had a little too much to drink as regards driving my car."

Suddenly Ella kissed Vincent softly on his lips, then her kiss hardened as Vincent kissed her back and as the couple held each other in a warm loving embrace they began to drift up towards the stars…

They were turning slowly in the night air.

Vincent did not realise what was happening at first as his only thought was of Ella…

Higher they went…

The soft breeze of the night was like a cosy blanket around them and when Vincent's eyes finally opened the two lovers were turning like a slow spinning top over the farm fields below.

"My God… we are… flying!"

"Yes Vincent, it is my Luxar gift, Charles has the same ability."

"To fly like Superman?"

Ella laughed, "No, not like Superman, only for short distance unless we fly up into the jetstream and only at night or if the clouds obscure the light of the sun… we can lighten our metabolism and control the airwaves around our bodies, drift or move swiftly with the air current."

"That is… just so cool, so where are we going Supergirl?"

"To your house Starry Night, like I said Vincent, the night is not over yet."

Ella kissed Vincent hard and this time there was an urgency to the kiss.

That night while Vincent and Ella made love…
Vaag was devouring Janet Eastley.

BULMER

From Eastley's house, Bulmer and Davis drove straight to the Roker Marina and boarded the Roker Seabird. The boat was now under constant police surveillance with one officer on guard, the forensic team had left but what interested Bulmer now were the laptop computers and phones of the small crew, none of which had been removed yet. Bulmer noticed Rolf's camera in Cathy Rolf's cabin.

"Okay Bob, you get the laptops and I'll get the phones and this camera, looks like someone was a keen photographer. We need to check all these pronto, looks like another late night bud."

Davis groaned but he knew that Bulmer was right, it was routine police work and something that had to be done.

By ten thirty pm both detectives had completed their research, it was now time for a coffee and a chat. Bulmer was the first to speak...

"Nothing on the phones Bob" he said hesitantly and then he continued, "But look at this will ya man."

Bulmer had plugged Rolf's camera into his desk computer and the look on Davis' face said it all.

"What the fucking Hell is that?"

"You tell me Bob, looks like something out of a horror movie doesn't it?"

"Do you... think that it is another victim Bull, like Salty Laing and Cathy Rolf?"

"I don't know Bob, the thing has got no skin by the look of it."

They were looking at the picture of Vaag on the stone altar just before he sat up.

"Where was this taken?"

"I was hoping that you could tell me, there is no location details of the jpeg, probably because it was taken inside a building. It is the last picture on Rolf's camera, looks like he was on some fucking creepy deserted island though full of old skulls and skeletons and again the locations have come up zero, it is as if this place does not exist" said Rolf as he backtracked through Rolf's pictures. Davis went to his desk to access Salty Laing's log of the Roker Seabird.

"Looks like their last stop was near to some island called Vaaga, off the Western Sahara coast… and this island does have some scary shit history man."

"Oh" said Bulmer who had now joined him, "What like?"

"Like the island was inhabited by cannibals for hundreds of years, seafaring bastards known as the Vaagen. Fuck me Bull, where is this investigation going?"

"To fucking Hell I think Bob… take a look at this man."

Bulmer then displayed the recent pages of research on Lucifer that Vaag had completed as Rolf.

"Dear God, why would Rolf want to know all that about the Devil?"

Both detectives looked at each other, it was late now in police HQ and both men were now feeling tired.

"Like I said earlier Bull, this whole thing is beginning to freak me out, is is somehow linked to Devil worship?"

"God knows Bob… look, it's late now, tomorrow we will see if forensics can come up with anything else; maybe you can find out more about Rolf first, we need to think about where he could possibly be."

"And what are you going to do Bull?"

"I think… I am going to try and find out more about that island called Vaaga."

EASTLEY

After Bulmer and Davis had left Eastley's house, Vaag went back to the garden to finish his drink. The two policemen had intrigued him, Vaag knew that the discarded skins of Salty Laing and Cathy Rolf would be a puzzle for them and this made him smile but Vaag now realised that he had to be ore careful with the remains of his meals in this new world and he was now thankful that Eastley's skin had slipped away into the waters of the sea to be most likely eaten by fish and other sea life. These were not trivial thoughts for Vaag, he knew that he needed something to take his mind off them.. He decided to go through Eastley's diary again.

Vaag began to make a mental list of possible first contacts then he came to the name Doctor Charles Richarde and this immediately interested him… *A doctor?* he thought, *surely the world of medicine had advanced greatly, the witch doctors and medicine men of my days were bound to be long gone?*

Vaag then checked the days of Eastley's diary and noticed that on Friday she had a late appointment to see Doctor Richarde at 9.45pm. *This doctor keeps late hours, I wonder why?* Vaag then accessed Eastley's memories it seemed that this Richarde was a doctor of the mind and Eastley was seeing him for something known as 'depression' due to the breakup of her marriage.

Vaag decided that he wanted to see this night doctor so he went to the kitchen for Eastley's small portable communicator. This device fascinated Vaag greatly, a thin oblong object that came to life at the touch of a button. Vaag knew that it was a smaller version of the computers he had learnt how to use on the Roker Seabird but he still found it unbelievable that all the knowledge of the world could be found by the All Knowing Google that lived inside this mobile phone communicator, *very much like a Genie in a bottle* he realised then he pondered, *Would this Mighty Google rule the world one day?* Vaag instantly concluded that it was indeed a possibility, when the Genie had finally managed to escape from the bottle.

Vaag phoned Richarde's number but it was an automated reply, all Vaag had to do was confirm that he was attending the appointment which he did. He then went back to the garden to relax in the sun. Vaag knew that his choice of food had been good, lucky perhaps but Eastley had been food that he had needed at the time. In this new environment, Vaag knew that his next choice of a meal would be crucial, he could not exist as Eastley forever. Richarde could be the first of his possible feasts and a doctor would have a viable habitat, one he could inhabit until his next need.

HOPEWOODPARK

Hopewood Park Hospital is a purpose built mental health hospital situated in Ryhope, Sunderland, next to the Ryhope Engines museum. Opened in 2014, the hospital is a modern and up to date facility with more than adequate parking but Vaag parked Eastley's Mercedes as close as he could to the hospital's main doors. The sun had just set as Vaag entered the spacious reception area. At this time of night the hospital was not busy and there was only one male receptionist on duty. Vaag asked to see Doctor Richarde and was told that Richarde's office was separate from the main building on the bottom boundary perimeter looking out to the sea.

Of course thought Vaag as he checked through Eastley' memory bank.

"I would advise you to drive down there, shall I show you where it is?" asked the receptionist.

"No, I now know where it is" replied Vag and he turned and walked out of the reception. This reply puzzled the receptionist but he just shrugged his shoulders then returned to reading his Uncut rock magazine.

Vaag returned to his car and proceeded to drive down the narrow road which led to Richarde's isolated office. The small one level building was partially surrounded by trees but as Vaag approached it he realised that he could see and smell the sea. The salt air always invigorated Vaag and as he entered Richarde's building he knew that he was the only one there.

Vaag was dressed sensually in a thin black leather jacket, tight black jeans and low heeled leather boots as he had no affection whatsoever now for high heel shoes. He had no bag and no phone communicator. Vaag took a seat outside of Richarde's office which had his name on the door. A few minutes later he was joined by Richarde.

"I am so sorry that I am slightly late Janet, I just had to check on something quickly in the main hospital."

"No problem at all doctor, I have only just arrived myself."

"Good, come through to my room please."

Vaag followed Richarde into his office and was pleasantly surprised by how spacious it was. There were two wide windows which had horizontal blinds and on the window facing the trees to the right of the building the blinds were drawn closed but on the other window which faced the sea they were open and the emerging moon peered nervously into the room.

Vaag sat on a comfortable leather chair facing Richarde who was dressed smartly in a dark blue suit and a white spotted navy tie. In between Vaag and Richarde was a low wood and glass coffee table on which there was a thin vase of red flowers and a classical music magazine.

"You have a nice view of the sea from here doctor" noted Vaag who smiled warmly at Richarde. He had made an effort to apply facial make-up to Eastley's face and he had been quite pleased with the result, it did not look like a young girl had applied it.

"That is a strange thing you say Janet" was Richarde's odd reply.

"How so doctor?"

"You have not called me doctor for some time and you have seen the view on many occasions."

"Oh… we are friends then?"

This reply by Vaag immediately puzzled Richarde and he did think that he noticed a difference in Eastley's voice, a definite lower tone.

"I would like to think that we are friends now Janet. How have you been, it has been a few weeks since your last appointment?"

"A lot can happen in a few weeks" Vaag said almost dreamily as he looked out to sea, imagining his island that he had left behind now.

"Indeed it can Janet… I sense that something has happened to you?"

Vaag's thoughtful expression suddenly changed as he turned and looked Richarde directly in the eye.

"Why do you say that doctor?"

"Not sure really… it's just that you… sound different I think."

Vaag shuffled in his chair, he had to remember that this was a doctor of the mind he was conversing with.

"Maybe… I have changed for the better doctor, maybe I do not really have to be here with you?"

Richarde thought for a moment before replying…

"That is the object of my work Janet, it has been a few years since your first appointment with me, a long struggle with your fight against depression and anxiety."

"And now that I am no longer depressed doctor, so where does that leave us?"

"Us?"

Vaag smiled, "You do not know how much Eastley craved for you, do you?"

"Eastley?"

Vaag almost bit his lip, he knew that he had been careless with his tongue, "Surely you knew?" he quickly added.

Richarde's senses heightened suddenly, he looked deeply into the eye of Eastley but he could not see her soul there… some Malos were capable of hypnotising their victims, possessing and controlling them like puppets.

The woman sitting in front of me is not the woman I know he immediately thought. Richarde became instantly cautious, he began to imagine that this was some Malos trick and yet he and his Luxstone ring could sense no Malos nearby. He returned to the conversation.

"I know that you cared for me… but not like that Janet."

"Yes, that would be improper, doctor patient rules I realise now… personally it would not bother me."

Once again it sounded like Eastley was talking about someone else. Richarde suddenly stood up…

"A drink Janet maybe, then we can discuss this further."

"Yes doctor, that would be nice."

Richarde went to the adjoining back room then returned with two glasses of tonic water with ice.

"No alcohol Charles, you disappoint me."

Getting the drinks was an excuse for Richarde to get closer to Eastley, to inhale her perfume, to get past the scent and smell her real odour.

Richarde returned to his seat and tried to compose himself. Eastley's scent was her scent, it was not offensive; in fact it was almost intoxicating and enticing…

And it was not a human odour.

Unknown to Richarde, Vaag had come to the same conclusion about him, his scent and the unusual sheen of his skin which was probably unnoticeable to most humans under the cloak of night.

This revelation really excited Vaag. He now wanted to know exactly who and what Doctor Charles Richarde really was. Vaag decided that he would try and trick Richarde into revealing his true identity. Abruptly he stood up and said, "Well Charles, I really must be going now."

Richarde was surprised by this, he had hoped to pry the truth from Eastley with conversation.

"Er… yes, it is getting late Janet, maybe we can continue our discussion at your next appointment. Let me show you out."

Vaag stepped out of the isolated office into the cool of the lonely night and Richarde followed hesitantly.

"The moon is beautiful tonight Charles is it not?" Vaag said and as he looked up to the sky he noticed a small camera above the office door. Vaag now knew that this was something that would record activities so he walked slowly away to the side of the office that faced the sea. Richarde followed him.

"I love the sea, don't you Charles? The sensual roll of the waves, back and forth, in and out, always arouse me."

"Yes, I love the sea Janet... but why do you say all this?" Richarde said and he was now standing close to Vaag.

"Because... I want to kiss you."

Vaag moved Eastley's hypnotic beautiful face and mouth towards Richarde but with a preternatural speed Richarde moved away from Vaag avoiding his deadly lips.

Vaag smiled, "You are not human are you doctor? I see that your skin has changed in the moonlight."

"It has hardened, I have hardened it because you are not Janet Eastley, not the Janet I know... I know not what you are, do you you serve The Malos?"

Vaag laughed, "I have no idea what a Malos is, if my old Latin knowledge serves me correctly it means Dark Ones?"

"Yes, Dark Ones, are you a Dark One?"

"I am Vaag, The Bone Drinker, The One of Many Faces, the only one of my kind... and I search for others like me."

Richarde had to compose himself, he knew that he was in the presence of something unknown and ancient; something he instinctively felt threatened by.

"I am not like you" Richarde stated immediately.

"No, you are not doctor, if you are not human then what are you?"

"I am Luxar, protector of humans from The Malos."

"How gallant, how heroic that sounds."

"And what of the human Eastley, what has happened to her, how is it that you look exactly like her?"

"I had to feed upon her, I needed her body and what was within it."

"She is dead then?"

"She lives inside of me, her memories and me are one now."

"She is dead within you" Richarde said bluntly.

"I suppose so if you put it like that... and what do you feed upon, I sense that human food and sustenance is not enough for you."

"Blood... the blood of animals."

"Poor animals then... but it is not enough is it, you crave human blood do you not?"

"The blood of animals is enough for me, it has been since the start of my existence."

"Maybe you need a new existence then?"

Vaag sprung at Richarde and grabbed him by the throat sending him crashing against the office wall and causing bricks to crush. Richarde's skin hardened further until it was as white as marble.

"Your stone skin is a wondrous defence Richarde and you are strong but not as strong as me… you will make a good joining."

Suddenly, to Vaag's surprise, Richarde's skin softened as his feet left the ground….

Vaag was no longer strangling Richarde, he was clinging onto him as they both headed up into the night sky.

Vaag gasped, "You have the power of flight… perfect!"

"Perfect indeed" growled Richarde baring his sharp Luxar teeth at Vaag with menace.

Vaag suddenly realised what Richarde was doing as the world below began to get smaller and smaller. Vaag's body, whatever the appearance was, was strong and robust but he knew that even he may not survive a fall from a great height… he released his grip immediately and plummeted downward like a human stone towards the ground behind Richarde's office.

Vaag landed deep onto the grass and soil but he was still alive, he did not move however, it was a ploy to fool Richarde… and it worked. Richarde swooped down and stood over the motionless Vaag.

"Whoever took your body Janet, no longer lives now" Richarde declared triumphantly.

Suddenly Vaag rolled over and grabbed the back of Richarde's head…

"Vaag will live forever, even the Devil Lucifer Himself could not kill me!"

Richarde's body did not have time to harden again as Vaag's elongated mouth clamped hard over Richarde's mouth.

The green acid flowed instantly with great speed from Vaag's body into Richarde's body causing Richarde to stagger back in shock.

"Do not fight it Doctor Richarde, soon you will be with me, inside me… together we will be invincible, as strong as the Fallen Angel himself."

Richarde fell back onto the soft grass as the acid flowed quickly throughout his body, turning his insides to liquid.

"Ella.. Ella… forgive me" were the last words Richarde uttered.

Vaag kneeled down beside Richarde and his mouth covered the fallen doctor's mouth. As Vaag sucked the remaining life from Richarde he immediately felt the power of the Luxar flow through him.

"I am a God now!" he declared, "Nothing will stop me in my search for my kind."

It was not an idle boast, Vaag now had the added power of Richarde his marble skin and his power of flight… *Who can defeat me?* he thought as his body turned into the body of Richarde.

Vaag stood up and looked at the clothing of Eastley he was still wearing which were now comically too tight for him. Instinctively he looked around but of course he was completely alone, he then removed Eastley's clothes and replaced them with Richarde's. Then Vaag looked down at the withered skin of Richarde that was lying on the grass. In the distant past, Vaag's food skins were removed by servants who were actually allowed to devour them as a reward but now he was thinking about policeman Bulmer and his petty investigation. Vaag was compelled to do something completely at odds with his character, he decided to hide Richarde's skin and Eastley's ripped clothes in the boot of Eastley's Mercedes.

Just before Vaag started the car, the face of Ella Newman suddenly flashed in Vaag's mind and an image of Moonlux Manor.

"Richarde's residence" Vaag muttered to himself, "That woman lives with him… but I cannot go there yet."

Vaag drove slowly away from Richarde's office towards Eastley's house in Whitburn, slightly irritated with himself because he really wanted to fly there.

ELLA

At the same time that Vaag was talking to Charles Richarde at Hopewood Park Hospital, Ella and Vincent were enjoying a drink in the city of Sunderland. They were sitting on the terrace of the Boar's Head Hotel which had stunning views of the River Wear as it wound it's way from the Durham countryside to the sea. The Boar's Head was situated on High Street West in an area of Sunderland called Hendon which was near the mouth of the Wear as it embraced the sea. Hendon was one of the dock areas of Sunderland but sadly the local shipping industry had seen a decline in recent years. Sunderland was once a thriving port, famous for it's shipyards, finally building highly technical deep sea exploration ships that could not be built anywhere else in the world. Sadly though, Margaret Thatcher's conservative government had decided to decimate the industry, some shipyards did survive but the area was nowhere near the force it had once been.

Vincent was looking up river to the Wearmouth Bridge and admiring the colours of the setting sun that were shining through it. He took a picture of the scene on his mobile phone.

"This will make a great painting I think" he said to Ella who turned to view the bridge.

"It is quite beautiful Vincent, this has always been my favourite time of the day, you should paint this view."

Vincent took another photograph but this time he included Ella in the shot.

"The bridge and you" he smiled, "A reminder of tonight."

Ella seemed to blush, "You are such a romantic Vincent" she said sweetly.

"And that is why you like me isn't it?"

"Yes, I suppose it is, at least one of the reasons, that and your artistic eyes I guess."

The terrace was full, all the tables were taken and in the centre of the terrace was a table that housed a square open fire which had just been lit, *a nice idea* thought Vincent as it not only provided heat on chilly evenings, it also added a serene ambience to the setting. Ella seemed to be daydreaming as she looked down towards the calm waters of the river.

"A penny for them" said Vincent as he sipped his Swedish Blonde Maxim ale.

"Hmn?"

Ella turned towards Vincent, her eyes reflecting the lively hungry flames of the newly lit fire.

"I was just… remembering"

"Remembering what?"

"How the river was… the clipper ships full of exotic cargo, the sailing yachts, the coal barges, the rowing boats... this was a bustling lively river once."

Vincent knew that Ella was now deep in the past.

"You have been here before then, in other times?"

"Oh yes, I cannot remember what this place was originally but I do remember it becoming a riverside inn in 1792. It was called the Mason's Arms then and Charles and I attended it's opening gala, it was a gay night and a wonderful party. I think it changed it's name to the Boar's Head sometime during the 1830's."

Vincent had to laugh at Ella's somewhat surreal words, "Y'know, you would make a great guide for a Sunderland pub crawl."

Ella laughed too, "Yes, I think I would and not many cities will have a tour guide aged 315, that's for sure!"

Vincent noticed that a woman on a nearby table had caught the tail end of what Ella had just said and the look on the woman's face was priceless, he thought that this was hilarious and caused his beer to go down the wrong way.

"Don't choke on your Swedish Blonde Vincent" Ella said and this comment made Vincent laugh even louder. Ella patted him sternly on the back until he began to breathe better. Some of the people on the nearby tables were showing concern for Vincent but he was a little worried about the woman who had been listening to their conversation.

"She heard what you said" whispered Vincent.

"Who did?"

"One of those women."

"What did she hear?"

"What you said about your age."

"I think the music would have drowned out most of my words, don't you think Vincent?"

The music playing on the terrace was louder now than when they had first entered the Boar's Head, the management seemed to be playing hits from every decade and at that moment they were playing Bryan Ferry's version of Bob Dylan's A Hard Rain's A-Gonna Fall which had been a big hit for Ferry in the seventies.

Vincent began to smile again then he said to Ella, "I still think that Charles does look a little like Bryan Ferry…"

"Roxy Music?"

"Yes, that Ferry… and also Doctor Strange."

"From the Marvel movie?"

"Yes, the magic guy."

It was Ella's turn to laugh out loud, "Yes Vincent, I think you are right, Charles does look a bit like both of them, I must tell him… he is kind of magic I guess, not sure about him singing rock songs though."

And again the two lovers began to laugh together and then Ella had to add, "I had a drink with Bryan Ferry once, and the brilliant drummer Paul Thompson after one of their concerts in Newcastle."

"You didn't…"

Ella did not know what Vincent meant at first then she realised and began to blush slightly.

"Of course not! Both are complete gentlemen. Actually, Bryan wanted to photograph me for one of their album covers."

"Wow, you could have been a Roxy girl then?"

"I might have been but Charles did not approve at the time, he was worried about the exposure or something, I guess he was right, we have to shun any kind of limelight; it would cause complications."

"That would have been real cool though."

"Yes, it would have, I definitely would have been the oldest art rock model in the world and nobody would have realised it."

Vincent began to laugh again, relieved that the nosy woman next to them could not hear what Ella had just said… then suddenly Vincent stopped laughing, Ella was quick to note that something had caught his eye…

"Oh no, I didn't know that she drank here, she usually drinks in Newcastle" Vincent remarked sounding instantly depressed.

Walking slowly towards the couple was Vincent's ex-girlfriend, she was with a tall muscular man and she seemed quite drunk. As she neared Vincent and Ella's table she blurted out…

"Well well… the Sunderland Vampire… and a friend. You better watch yourself pet mind, he bites!"

Vincent's old girlfriend was referring to the last time she was with Vincent, when he had suffered a psychotic episode triggered by his involvement with the spirits of Whitby… Vincent had actually bit her neck believing that he was a vampire, during that moment he had been possessed, totally unaware of what he was doing.

"Look Candice… I could tell you why that happened but I know that you would not believe me… and you didn't actually believe in me or support me afterwards did you?"

Candice laughed loudly causing the drink in her hand to spill onto the wood panelled floor.

"Do you really think that I would want to continue to see a man who thought that he was… a vampire! Haway man, I'm not as mad as you am I?."

Vincent just looked down into his glass of beer, he did not want to remember this episode in his life and Ella knew it, she also knew that the tall man was looking suddenly agitated.

"So this is the mad bastard?" he said then he began to step towards Vincent, his drunken eyes glaring with alcohol fuelled hate.

In a flash Ella stood up and grabbed the man's arm and looked him directly in the eyes. It was obvious that the man was now in pain.

"I think that you have had too much to drink don't you? You seem to be spoiling my night and I just want you both to know that I bite too!"

The big man staggered back, the strength of Ella's grip had astounded him and he certainly did not like the look in Ella's brown eyes that seemed to be reflecting the flames of the terrace fire. Candice saw the obvious fear in her boyfriend's eyes and quickly decided to leave the Boar's Head, "C'mon pet, let's get out of here. it's full of fucking weirdos… she probably thinks she's a vampire too."

"A Luxar…" whispered Ella into Candice's ear and she knew that only Candice could hear her.

A mystified Candice and her somewhat confused man turned and walked away as quick as they could. The terrace music was now The Rolling Stones' Sympathy For The Devil and Ella spontaneously began to dance sensually and seductively in front of Vincent…

"C'mon Vincent, forget that stupid bitch and that big idiot, I feel like dancing."

One or two other people on the terrace inspired by Ella, began to dance too and suddenly there was a party atmosphere. Vincent stood up and grabbed Ella tightly as they swayed to the hypnotic beat of The Stones.

"Ella, you are an absolute marvel."

"Captain Marvel the super hero? I thought I was Supergirl?"

"Yes, that is who you look like, Captain Marvel."

"Oh, glad we cleared that up then."

And they both laughed again.

After the Boar's Head closed, Vincent and Ella went night clubbing and danced and grooved the night away, totally unaware of what was happening to Charles Richarde.

RICHARDE

Driving back to Janet Eastley's house in Whitburn as Doctor Charles Richarde, Vaag began to see more intermittent images of Richarde's memories as they flashed through his mind… the woman called Ella Newman, the old mansion called Moonlux Manor and where exactly it was in the Ryhope countryside. At one point he was tempted to turn the car around and go there, to see his new home and to find out who this woman called Ella was. But he knew that his assimilation of Richarde was not complete, it would take time before all of Richarde's memories had settled comfortably in his mind therefore the sensible thing to do was to go to Eastley's house until the transformation was complete. Also, he knew that that the clock was ticking, it would not be long before those that knew Eastley realised that she was missing.

In Eastley's house, Vaag looked at his new body in the long vertical mirror that hung in the hallway. Vaag was impressed, here was a man that looked in his mid-forties, tall and and handsome with thick black hair and hooded blue eyes, the hair that was white at the sides gave a distinguished look. Vaag suddenly realised that Eastley obviously had no male clothes in her closets so that prompted the decision to relocate to Moonlux Manor at some point the next day. But the night was still young and Vaag was beginning to feel a new craving, the craving for human blood.

Richarde lied to me thought Vaag as he stood in Eastley's garden staring at the moon, *he did crave human blood but he suppressed it for all those years, how admirable of you Charles but I am not so chivalrous… and your power of flight is an intoxicating thought.*

Vaag felt his metabolism harden then lighten by the power of thought… and slowly he could feel the the air around him that seemed like a living entity now that was caressing him sensually, air that he could now control, both his hands seemed to touch the ground, push the ground but it was the night air, propelling him upwards, up above Eastley's house and the village of Whitburn. Vaag could see people in the distance, coming out of The Jolly Sailor pub, but the streets were not full though and Vaag was glad of this, he did not want any human videoing him on their phone communicator and putting the images of it on the thing called the internet.

Vaag was quite high now and he was pleased that Richarde's suit was dark blue, he knew that he must have been almost undetectable to the human eye. He checked Richarde's memories to see if there was any power of invisibility but was disappointed to realise that there was no such ability available to him. Still, Vaag knew that his considerable strength had increased ten fold and that with Richarde's power of flight meant that surely Vaag was now a match for Lucifer should he ever have to confront him again.

Then suddenly Vaag saw Richarde's original home of Terralux in his mind, his parents, his family, the Elders that had recruited him to become a Human Protector but he quickly dismissed these thoughts from his mind, at the moment they held no interest for him, the only thing that he could think about and focus on was human blood.

Vaag had drifted southward, he was now over the large sea structure that was known as Marsden Rock. The tide was out and the beach was deserted except for two young lovers that were caressing each on the lonely damp sand.

"Young humans having sex" Vaag muttered to himself, "How amusing and arousing. I think will let them copulate, let them enjoy their last night under this bright moon… then they will be mine."

Vaag watched the couple as they made passionate love and when the young man rolled off the sweating panting body of his girlfriend, Vaag began to slowly descend towards them, his body vertical with the ground.

It was the young man who saw Vaag first…

"What… the fuck is that?"

"Is what?" echoed his mystified girlfriend.

"That figure in the moonlight… coming down toward us."

"You said you wouldn't smoke it again" growled the young girl.

"I haven't" replied her boyfriend who was now sitting up… but before he could say anything else Vaag was upon him.

The girl screamed and instinctively tried to roll away but Vaag held her with his control of the air, she felt like she was in the grip of a giant invisible hand, fingers that were covering her mouth so that she could not scream any longer.

While the air that Vaag controlled held the girl tight and still and caressed her between the legs, Vaag sunk his sharp Luxar teeth into the neck of the disbelieving young man who had succumbed to shock by what was happening… when he finally tried to fight back and defend himself it was too late, Vaag was in the process of sucking every drop of blood from him.

Vaag's eyes were now totally red as the blood of the man flowed into him… but he was not finished, not fully satisfied. The girl's eyes turned in fear to Vaag as he slowly hovered toward her.

"Do not be afraid my pretty, it will not take long. Your blood will soon flow with mine and you will feel ecstasy like you have never known before or will ever know again as my sensual invisible touch arouses you to another climax."

Within minutes the young couple lay dead together, side by side, both completely drained of their blood so that they looked like grisly withered pale skeletons and Vaag felt full and satisfied, it was almost as good as his normal acidic feed and his body had been re-nourished completely.

I could feed like this forever thought Vaag and this appealed to him because the combined strength of himself and Richarde was immense, something he would find hard to give up. Then he thought about disposing of the two human bodies but as he looked around at the deserted beach and the silent waters that were approaching, he concluded, *Let the tide take them, my offering to the gods of the sea. By daylight they will be gone.*

But Vaag was both right and wrong.

The water did take them but returned them on the morning tide, to be discovered by a man and his dog during their early morning walk along the beach.

BULMER

It was 7.30 in the morning when Detective Davis phoned Bulmer the next day.

"Morning Bull, I came into work early today and I have just been informed of two murders on Marsden beach, not far from the Grotto."

"Damn… not like Salty Laing and Cathy Rolf I hope?"

Davis went quiet for a moment.

"I… think they're similar Bull."

"Similar what do you mean Bob?"

"This time only their blood is missing."

"What?"

"This does sound like a fucking vampire Bull."

"Bloody Hell man, what the fuck is going on around here… look, I'll meet you there within the hour."

***

Marsden Grotto is a unique pub, set within the cliff-side and is only accessible by a long set of steep wooden steps or by a lift at the top of the cliff. Thankfully for Bulmer the lift was working because the pub manager had been alerted by what had happened.

The sun was rising and it was a dry day but there was an early morning chill wind blowing in from the sea. The bodies had been covered by a large forensics tent and when Bulmer entered the tent, Davis was already inside.

"Hi Bull… looks like we've got another gruesome case on our hands" Davis said looking down at the remains of the young couple on the sand.

"Fuck me man, what kind of monster did this?"

Davis was standing next to the forensics doctor who knew Bulmer well.

"In all my years of doing this job, I have never seen anything like this. I have heard reports though from colleagues of something similar but that was years ago."

Bulmer looked at the doctor thoughtfully.

"I would like to see those reports Doc, it that is possible?"

"It might take some time to find them, they're probably not on the computer, it was that long ago."

"The nineties, eighties?"

"Possibly, but definitely before that Bull, the seventies and late sixties… I think there were cases in Scotland after that and they will be a lot harder to get but I will see what I can dig up for you."

"Whatever you do, don't dig up fucking Dracula will you!"

Davis and the forensics doctor chuckled but Bulmer had struck a chord, there was something evil and vampiric about the two murders on Marsden beach.

"Okay Bob, we'll see what forensics can come up with these two but I've got a feeling that they will be stumped just like the Roker Marina murders."

The forensic doctor felt like he had to reply to what Bulmer had said.

"We deal in facts Bull, just like you, what you get from us is what happened to the victims and maybe how, the next bit is up to you."

"Okay Doc, I get what you're saying but these murders are hardly run of the mill are they?"

"You think they are murders then Bull?" asked Davis and he knew that his question sounded somewhat pathetic.

"What else can they be Bob?"

"I… was just thinking… maybe an animal or something is to blame for this?"

"Alright Bob, I get what you are saying… look, we need to get back to the station for a briefing and debriefing, I tell you what though, I think that the two cases are connected somehow and for me the trail leads back to that island called Vaaga."

As the two stepped out of the forensic covering they were greeted by a news reporter.

"Hi there Bull, glad to see you're on the case."

"Fuck me, didn't take you long to get here Jonesy."

"I was here at seven thirty Bull, the guy who found the bodies phoned the paper after the police, I've just finished interviewing the poor guy. Strange thing we've got here Bull, do you think that they are related to the Marina murders?"

"You obviously know all about that too then?"

"Of course, my story is breaking at midday about it, creepy empty human skins, this will go national immediately."

"Damn!" exclaimed Bulmer but he knew that it was inevitable, something that weird could not be bottled up for long.

"So what do you think Bull, a virus, or maybe some sort of parasite is causing this?"

"Look Jonesy, you should know that nothing like that has been confirmed, it has virtually been ruled out; we don't want the public to panic so I hope that is in your report."

"It is Bull."

"Good, then there is nothing more to say."

"How about a murderer who is somehow mimicking a vampire?"

"No fucking comment Jonesy!"

Bulmer brushed past Jones, he could feel his blood pressure rising, he knew that whatever was happening was beginning to get to him.

"Haway Bob, we've got work to do, we'll leave the press to their vampires and bogeymen."

But before Bulmer got into the lift that would take the two detectives to the top of the cliff and the car-park, he had to say to Davis, "I've just decided something Bob."

"What's that Bull?"

"I'm going to that island Bob, I'm going to get approval when we get back to HQ then book my tickets."

"And me?"

"You need to stop here and head up the cases till I get back, sorry to do this but I have to go to Vaaga, to see what Rolf saw."

"I understand Bull... the shit will hit sure the fan at dinnertime, so they're gonna ask what we are doing."

"We can't stop the news getting out, especially with something like this but we can only do our best to try and find out just what the fuck is going on. I know that there is a difference in the murders but they are just so damned similar when you think about it."

"They are Bull... and it does seem to be some sort of cannibalistic vampirism and I can't believe that I have just said that!"

"And that fucking island has had more than it's fair share of bloody cannibals, that's for sure!"

Davis laughed but his throat was dry.

HARPER

Vincent Harper opened his eyes and turned to look at Ella who was sleeping still on his wide king-size bed in his house Starry Night. He felt like he was in a dream, lying next to the most beautiful woman he had ever known or seen.

Vincent looked at his watch, 9.33 in the morning but he had no desire to get out of bed. The night had been perfect, when Vincent was lovingly inside of Ella, it felt like he was inside her mind. He had seen flashing images of her, of her past, of her life with Richarde, it may have just been his imagination but he knew that he had made some sort of mental connection which was like nothing he had experienced before, it was like true love had joined them completely together as one.

Vincent gently stroked the side of Ella's face and then he brushed her hair softly from her eyes. Slowly and sensually his hands moved down her neck to her shoulders and then to her breasts and her taut erect nipples. He thought that he heard her moan but he was not sure. Vincent's hand moved across her lithe stomach and then down between her legs where she was moist and warm…

Ella's eyes opened slowly.

"Vincent… come to me" she murmured sexually and Vincent's hard erect penis entered her from the side like a living thing that had been given permission to go to some sort of bodily Heaven.

Once again, Vincent immediately felt like he was flying as he moved slowly within her, gentle but urgent at the same time…

And time disappeared
It was as if he was above the Earth
In the Heavens
Pure white clouds drifting by him
As they moved together in ecstasy
Climbing higher towards the stars
As they both approached climax

And when they both came together
It was as if the Heavens had opened
And comets were flashing across them
In the colours of the rainbow
They were in another place now
The place where hearts come together
Vincent rolled onto his side and out of Ella
It was a parting that now seemed unnatural
Something unwanted
Both looked at each other and all they could do was smile.

Then Vincent seemed to drift away, to sleep again and it was only the singing of the birds in his garden that awakened him. It was now late in the morning and as he opened his eyes again, Ella was standing before him fully dressed.

"I must go Vincent, Charles will be wondering where I am."

"You're a grown woman Ella…"

"Yes but he will be worrying about me, he always has."

Vincent laughed, he knew that there was nothing in the world that Ella should be afraid of… what he he did not know was that this thought of his was soon about to change.

"Okay, I'll get ready and take you."

"No, my car is here remember? Look, I will phone you later, maybe we can get a meal together?"

"Or maybe a takeaway and a movie?"

"Yes, I would like that."

Ella kissed Vincent lovingly on the cheek then left the bedroom. Normally Vincent would have stopped in bed a little longer but now he was invigorated and full of energy, he decided that he would *have lunch or breakfast or brunch or whatever then I will start that painting of Ella and the Wearmouth Bridge.*

***

At midday, Vincent was eating bacon and eggs and watching the local news on the television in his kitchen. Suddenly the Roker Marina appeared on the screen announcing the fate of Salty Laing and Cathy Rolf and the disappearance of her husband Alan. Vincent stopped chewing his food as the gruesome details were revealed.

"My God, what the Hell has happened there?" Vincent muttered to himself.

And then the same reporter was standing on Marsden beach talking about the discovery of two bloodless victims… Vincent nearly choked on his bacon, the reporter had mentioned 'vampirism' and immediately Vincent thought of Richarde and Ella and the dreaded Malos.

"Dear Lord… I better phone Ella!"

Vincent quickly dialled Ella's number on his mobile phone.

"Have you seen the news Ella?"

"No what has happened?"

Vincent sounded breathless.

"You need to check it out, I'm thinking that the Malos are involved!"

"What! Are you sure?"

"When you see what has happened, I think you'll understand."

"Then why has Charles not said anything to me?"

"Maybe he has not seen the news yet?"

"Maybe… I have just been talking with Charles in the conservatory and…"

"And what?"

"And something is bothering me."

"In what way?"

"I can't… look, I will look at the news then talk with Charles then I will phone you back later."

Vincent was now worried about Ella, suddenly that make-believe world of 'vampires' seemed all too real.

"Okay my love but be careful."

"It is what Charles and I are here for Vincent."

"And I am here for you" replied Vincent.

"I know that."

Then the phone call ended.

RICHARDE

Vaag had woken early from his dreamless sleep, his body was still vibrant from the blood of the two young humans. After showering he noticed the amount of blood on Richarde's clothes so he decided that he would go to Moonlux Manor without haste, leaving the mystery of Eastley's disappearance behind him. Vaag chuckled to himself as he stood in front of Eastley's Mercedes, more work for policemen Bulmer and Davis, *they will be quite the busy bees* he thought and he chuckled to himself, a moment of humorous thought that quickly turned into a full throttle laugh. He enjoyed playing cat and mouse with humans, he always had done, they were intelligent beings but also naive and gullible which had always proved their downfall throughout the years.

The gates to Eastley's home were open, her car was ready... but Vaag decided something on the spur of the moment, he decided that he would fly to Moonlux Manor and his new life there, this was surely more befitting a god like him.

Vaag was very intrigued about meeting the female Ella, maybe she could be his partner, his mate even? *Maybe I will be able to confide in her, she will have the same bloodlust as I so maybe I can persuade her to follow her true desires, maybe she will even learn to love me, so that then there will be no need to continue my search for my own kind.*

For Vaag, these thoughts were encouraging and wetted his appetite for Ella and Moonlux Manor. He noticed that the sun had hardened his skin which was now completely white. He also knew that both Richarde and Ella could not or would not fly when in this heavy state... but he was stronger, his control over the air much stronger than them and he began to hover slowly upwards.

See Richarde, see what power you have now!

Suddenly Vaag shot skyward like a human bullet until he was amongst the sparse clouds. The morning was hot and dry and in the distance he saw a large winged metal bird that he now knew was an aeroplane, it was approaching Newcastle Airport but this did not bother him because the metal bird was miles away. Vaag now knew that he had the eyes of a hawk and he pinpointed his destination along the coast of Sunderland, the Ryhope countryside and his new home which was called Moonlux Manor.

MOONLUX MANOR

It did not take Vaag long to reach his destination, even in his hardened state he could travel at great speed. Soon Vaag was standing in front of the large double doors to the historic mansion he now owned. He fumbled through his coat pockets until he found what he wanted, Richarde's keys, *The keys to my new kingdom* he thought with great satisfaction and once inside the impressive building he went straight to Richarde's living area in the Castle Tower and changed into fresh blue trousers and a clean white shirt, he decided that he would burn his bloodstained clothes later.

It was now mid-morning and Vaag decided that he would familiarise himself with his new abode even though his mind held all of Richarde's memories now. Vaag went from the tower through his recreational room that he knew was his personal domain then into the large banquet hall and then through into the adjoining semicircular conservatory to admire the beauty of the surrounding rear gardens.

Impressive, Richarde has the taste of a king, I am going to enjoy my stay here Vaag thought with glee…

Then suddenly he sensed a presence, the scent of the woman Ella who was once human. Ella had just entered the Manor and Vaag heard her calling Richarde's name. With a preternatural response, Vaag replied to Ella, his words drifting from the conservatory and the banquet hall to the hallway entrance in which Ella was standing….

"I am here Ella, in the conservatory, come and sit with me and enjoy the sun on your skin."

Ella walked down the wide hallway which displayed portraits of humans that Richarde had come to admire, then she went through the banquet hall that Hinks' wife had insisted Hinks built before their marriage, a hall that had large wide painted glass windows that were impressive as any cathedral then Ella stepped into the brightness of the large conservatory. Richarde was sitting at one of the large marble tables on one of the wide comfortable wicker chairs. His face was white and his eyes were blood red.

"Ah, sit with me my pretty and tell me where you have been."

Ella sat directly opposite Richarde and immediately she was puzzled by Charles calling her *pretty*, he had never called her that to her knowledge. As the sun's rays gently bathed Ella, her skin also turned to marble white.

"I have..."

For some strange reason, Ella did not want to mention Vincent or that she had stayed at Starry Night with him, there was no rational reason for this that she could think of, it seemed to be purely instinctive.

"I have been... to see my friend Alice."

Ella did have a friend called Alice. Alice Ashcroft was blind and like Ella she had been an orphan. Ella had met Alice at a hospital function in aid of homeless children and a friendship was formed instantly due to their similar backgrounds. Alice's handicap helped shield Ella's secret from her. Alice was now in her early forties and Ella pretended to be that age when she was with Alice. Ella so wanted to tell Alice the truth about her and had always thought that one day she would because Alice was one human that Ella could totally trust. In spite of her blindness, Alice was a sculptor and Ella was really looking forward to introducing her to Vincent. But now she was regretting mentioning her name to Richarde which was a very strange feeling. Richarde seemed to drift away for a moment as if lost in thought then suddenly he replied, "Ah yes, Alice, how is she?"

"She... she is fine, you know Alice, nothing ever gets her down."

"Indeed... a brave human I suspect, I am glad that you have a friend."

Human? Charles has never referred to Alice as a 'human' before...

Richarde was still facing the sun, basking in it like he was almost worshipping it.

"I love the sun, it is a shame that we have to hide away from it when we are with humans."

Charles is a strange mood thought Ella and then she thought that she noticed something unusual about him, his voice sounded slightly different, she was sure that it was somewhat deeper in tone.

"You seem, sort of distant today Charles, is something bothering you?"

Charles turned suddenly toward Ella, his facial expression stern as he looked Ella straight in the eyes.

"No... why do you say such a thing?"

Richarde seemed almost aggressive suddenly and this bothered Ella.

"You know that I care about you Charles and I know that sometimes your work with the hospital can take a toll on you."

"Yes, the hospital... I have decided to stop working there."

Ella was astounded by this abrupt unexpected statement, it was as if a shock-wave had suddenly struck her.

"What, leave the hospital, but why?"

"I have..." Richarde began and he suddenly seemed to be thinking seriously about this seemingly impulsive decision, "I have decided that I have been there too long now, the few people that know me there will begin to ask questions about my age and how I look."

Ella knew this to be true, his work there always had a time limit because of what he was.

"I thought that you had a few more years there until you 'retired'?"

"Yes… but now I want to devote all my time to…. my studies, yes, my studies" he repeated as if to justify his decision. Richarde had been writing manuscripts on the history of human medicine throughout the ages for years, focussing on mental health issues and the workings of the mind which Ella knew he always wanted to publish one day, something she encouraged him to do.

"Your history of medicine concerning the human brain?"

"Yes… that is right."

"Then I am pleased for you Charles and I do know how stressful your hospital work could be at times."

"Yes, there will be no more stress, I will make sure of that."

There was a chilling sound to Richarde's words which puzzled Ella again but she did not dwell on it.

"Then we must celebrate soon… another chapter opens up in your life."

"Another chapter has indeed opened up" grinned Richarde and for some reason Ella did not like the way that he was smiling at her.

"Look Charles, I need to go to my room and freshen up, we will talk later."

"I will look forward to that."

And once again Ella felt that Richarde's words did not seem right

***

After showering and while she was enjoying a cup of coffee, Ella received the phone call from Vincent regarding the news headlines. After she had finished talking to Vincent, Ella turned the news channel on…

"My God, I think Vincent is right, Malos have crossed through the Portal."

Ella hurried downstairs to Richarde's recreational room and found Richarde sitting in front of the large ornamental fireplace but no fire was burning. On the table to the right of him was a large wine glass full of blood. Richarde looked up to Ella, he was slightly concerned about the expression on her face.

"What is it Ella, there is a worried countenance on your face?"

"Have you seen the news Charles?"

"Yes, I have" Richarde replied calmly.

"Then you do not think that it is the work of the Malos?"

"Ah, the Malos…" Richarde murmured then he seemed to drift away for a moment as he looked down at the large sliver and white ring on the centre finger of his right hand…

There was a dark face against a tree

In pain

As if defeated

A dark light was surrounding this creature

A darkness that began to fade

As the white light from Richarde's Luxstone ring

pierced the creature's heart

The dark face had red eyes

Sharp red teeth

And bulging red veins

A Malos in a hardened state

And the Malos was defeated

Defeated by the immense power of Richarde's ring

Devoured by the white light almost

A blinding light that opened a portal to another reality…

"I have you Malos, you go back to Terralux to pay for your crimes now"

Richarde shouted in the night and only the Malos could hear him. Richarde stretched out his arm and fist in front of him and the beam of white light from his ring pushed the Malos through the darkness of the night into the portal…

Suddenly the white light faded as the portal slit closed.

"Begone and never return" Richarde declared and then suddenly he was back in the room with Ella who was repeating his name…

"Charles… Charles."

"I… was just remembering… I was somewhere else…"

"You do need to be somewhere else Charles, you need to be at Marsden beach so that your Luxstone ring can try and pick up the scent."

And as Ella said the word scent, it triggered something awkward within her… she suddenly realised that Charles did not smell the same… but there were now more serious matters at hand than Richarde's body odour.

"Yes, the scent… you are right my Ella, I must go there but first I will finish my drink."

Richarde opened his hand and the glass of blood levitated toward it and when he had the glass firmly in his hand, Richarde swallowed the blood in one go.

"Animal blood, not as good as human blood obviously but it will do for now."

Ella's mouth opened and she gasped quietly, not just at Richarde's words but because of what she had just seen. Her and Richarde's control of the air was never capable of such a thing, they could only control the air that was around them until they were up amongst the air currents that they could then ride like birds. What Richarde had done was akin to telekinesis, a power that he had certainly never displayed before.

This is not Charles… it cannot be thought Ella as she slowly backed away from him, careful as to not alerting him of any suspicions.

"I… will go… and check my computer… for any other news updates… I also think that I should go back to Alice, warn her to be careful about going out alone."

"Yes Ella, you do that and I will go the place called Marsden and see if this magnificent ring will react to anything" Richarde replied, once more admiring the white Luxstone on his clenched hand. As Ella turned Richarde said, "There is no need to worry my sexy young thing I will find and defeat this Malos creature by nightfall, you will see and then maybe we can 'celebrate' together?"

An icy chill surged through Ella, those words 'my sexy young thing' were definitely not something Richarde would say and *was he inferring that they sleep together? Surely not!* Ella had to leave, she had to go somewhere at once and that somewhere was Starry Night.

STARRY NIGHT

Back in her room, Ella packed two large sports bags and her laptop and other essentials and took them to her BMW which was still parked at the front of Moonlux Manor, she assumed that Richarde had left for Marsden beach but she was still wary, she did not want Richarde to see the bags, she looked back at all the windows but she could not see Richarde. Ella had no need to worry though, Richarde was still in his room supping fresh animal blood, he had no intention of going to Marsden, he was in fact concocting the story he would tell Ella later about how he had bravely defeated the Malos and then he began to think about how he would seduce her. Ella had suddenly become a sexual infatuation for Vaag and this was something he relished.

Ella was heading to see Vincent, to ask if she could stay there, she had decided not to tell Richarde where she was, if Richarde was not the real Richarde then maybe he did not know who Vincent was or maybe he did know but had no idea that they were lovers now? Ella was panicking, she needed Vincent now and as she stopped her car in front of Vincent's house she breathed out a heavy a sigh of relief.

Vincent was in his studio painting and Ella thought that he might be as she hurried around the side of the house. Vincent was having a coffee break as Ella entered the studio.

"Vincent, I am so glad that you are here!" Ella said emotionally as her arms went around him tightly.

"Whoa there… what's the matter now?" said Vincent who knew immediately that something was terribly wrong.

Ella held her head as if trying to think logically, "Can I park my car in your garage?"

"Sure, it's a double garage so there is plenty of room but why…"

"I will tell you everything when I get back" said Ella and she then kissed Vincent quickly on the cheek. Ella went to move her car and Vincent poured out two large gin and tonics. When Ella returned, Vincent told Ella to sit down at the table and chill out and that she was safe with him now.

"If only that was the case dear Vincent but yes, I do feel safer now."

"Okay honey, I think you better let it all out."

Ella took a large gulp of her drink then started…

"I… think Charles is not Charles" she abruptly declared.

"What?" gasped Vincent as this was not what he was expecting but he immediately thought that the Malos had something to do with it.

"Do you think that the Malos has something to do with this?"

"I… really don't know but I have come to the conclusion that somehow he has been possessed."

"What… by who or what?"

"The creature that killed the two people at the marina possibly?"

"Laing and … Rolf?"

"Yes… it does not seem to be the work of a Malos though, this is something I have never seen before."

"You, me and a million others… but what about the young couple on the beach, that sounds like Malos?"

"Yes it does, it is something that Charles could do…"

"My God… but what and how could something control Charles like that?"

"I do not know but what I am fairly certain of is that the Charles at Moonlux Manor now is not the Charles we know."

Ella then went on to tell Vincent everything about her recent discussion with Richarde, about the things he had said, of what he had inferred and how he had controlled the wine glass.

Vincent had to agree with what Ella was thinking but there was a question that was niggling at him, "The wine glass, you told me that you control the air around you, that is how you have the power of flight; could Charles not have developed this power even further?"

"Possibly, some ancient Luxar have this ability but I think Charles would have to be much older and stronger?"

"I… think you made the right decision to leave Moonlux, and obviously you can stay here as long as you like until we work out what we have to do."

"I… think I know what we have to do" said Ella suddenly, "but I will come to that later. Like I said, if Charles has somehow been possessed then he will possibly have no recollection of the two of us being friends?"

"Right, let's hope so, but wait, you have other friends…"

"Yes and I think my oldest and best friend could now be in danger soon… when I do not return, Charles or whatever he is might use her as leverage for me to return. I think he wants me Vincent, he wants me to be more than just a work partner."

"Over my dead body, the bastard!"

"And mine, unfortunately it might just come to that but like I said, I will tell you what I have planned later, first I think we have to get my friend here too if that is okay with you?"

"Of course, you know that Ella, who is she?"

"She is quite old by human standards, early forties I think, her name is Alice Ashcroft, she's a sculptor."

"Ashcroft? I know her work Ella, remarkable considering she has been blind since birth."

"It is good that you know about her, you both have a lot in common with your artwork. Can we go and see her now please?"

"Sure, we'll take my BMW Pickup."

RICHARDE

While Ella was informing Vincent about her unpleasant meeting with Charles Richarde, Vaag was sunbathing on a sturdy sun-bed on the flat roof of the Castle Tower. Vaag was fully naked and his skin was marble white from the harmful rays of the sun, his body was now heavy and the sun recliner barely held his weight as he looked skyward. He was still thinking about Ella and how he could charm her and win her over. He still thought that like Richarde, Ella still had a secret obsession, the craving for human blood…

That is it he suddenly thought, *I need to give her a human offering. Maybe a human that who would become a servant, someone we could drink from should we suddenly desire a nice glass of fresh warm blood.*

Vaag concluded that his idea was perfect as he stood up and went to the tower turrets to scour the local landscape. The Castle Tower was much higher than the rest of Moonlux Manor and had a 360 degree view of the countryside. He looked north towards Sunderland, to the bustling city first, a city that was forever trying to redefine itself. Vaag then looked east towards the sea and in the far distance he could see Hopewood Park Hospital, a place that Richarde would never return to now. He looked southward to the nearby coastal villages of Seaham and Horden and then he turned westward to the wide open fields of the Durham countryside. *To select a servant now, this will probably be the best area* he thought and with his new acute vision, he focussed on an abandoned overgrown railway line that humans now used as a pathway.

Not far from Moonlux Manor, Vaag spotted a young human female who was walking with her dog along the track. There were no other humans about.

"Perfect" Vaag exclaimed, "This day you will serve a higher purpose my pretty."

Vaag did not bother to clothe himself, *there is no time* he thought as he did not want the hindrance of human witnesses arriving on the scene. Vaag dived from the tower then flew upwards and headed at great speed towards the young girl like a determined bird of prey. Within minutes Vaag had swooped down in front of the girl who was video chatting with a friend on her phone…

Suddenly, standing in front of her was a tall man who was naked and totally white and the light that was being reflected from Vaag's body was almost blinding her. The marble vision before her spoke with a voice that sounded surreal, "Good, you are a black girl, I always loved the taste of black people."

"What the… who… are you?" the stunned girl stuttered. The girl's hand and phone had dropped to her side, her friend could now see the shimmering reflective light from the large white form of Vaag, she became instantly alarmed by this strange vision that had suddenly appeared before her friend.

"What is it Jenna, what the fuck is that!" the girl's friend screamed but Jenna was not listening, she was transfixed by the naked image of Vaag as she waited for his answer.

"I… am a god and you will worship me."

Suddenly Jenna's dog Benny, a small white terrier that had been slightly further down the track, came racing back to attack Vaag. Vaag turned and stamped on the annoying animal, crushing it immediately.

"No, no…" screamed Jenna and her phone dropped from her hand as she reached down to the flattened bloody mess that had been her beloved pet.

Vaag stood on Jenna's phone and so ended the video call; then he grabbed Jenna who was now in a complete state of shock and as Vaag flew up into the air she lost consciousness.

ALICE

Alice Ashcroft lived in an old farmhouse near to the Durham Cricket Club in the town of Chester-le-Street. Her studio and rear garden backed onto the banks of the River Wear as it lazily rolled its way towards Sunderland.

Alice was relaxing in her back garden when her mobile phone rang.

"Hi Alice, just checking that you are in."

"Oh, hi Ella, yes, I am enjoying the afternoon sun in the garden with Rocky."

"That's good, I… thought that I might call in, there is someone I want you to meet."

"Yeah of course, you can come here whenever you want, you know that."

"Okay, we're on our way."

Like Vincent had suggested, they took his car and within half an hour they were sitting beside Alice at her garden table. After Ella had introduced Vincent to Alice she was keen to learn more about him.

"So what do you do Vincent?" Alice asked as she sipped at the wine that Ella had brought.

"As little as possible" Vincent replied with humour then confidently added, "I am an artist, not as renowned as you but I try my best."

"Wait… are you Vincent Harper?"

Ella had not mentioned Vincent's surname.

"Yes?"

"I read reviews of your recent exhibition, they were wonderful."

"You read them?" replied Vincent then he felt like kicking himself for being so insensitive.

"Sorry, I meant that I listened to them on my computer."

"Of course I'm sorry."

"No need Vincent, your reaction was understandable."

Suddenly Alice became alarmed…

"Where's Rocky, has he wandered off?"

Rocky was Alice's guide dog, an intelligent cross Border Collie that was young and still quite inquisitive.

"He's down at the riverside, beside that guy who is fishing, he's playing with the guy's dog" said Vincent who was looking down toward the river bank.

"He doesn't normally wander off but he's a young dog, he will come back immediately if I call."

"I think it is a bitch that he is playing with" quipped Ella and they all laughed.

"I'll have a walk and get him, I want to see if that guy has caught anything."

Ella was sitting in the shade of a nearby tree wearing large sunglasses, she knew that the river fisherman was too far away to make out her white skin.

"Take your time Vincent" she said to him and he knew exactly what she meant, Ella wanted time to explain things to Alice and he knew that it would not be easy for her.

"Looks like you've nabbed yourself a good'un there Ella and somehow I sense that he is a bit younger than you?" said Alice as Vincent began to make his way slowly down towards the river bank.

"Just a little bit, he's my toy boy" replied Ella and both women laughed, "You know that I have never had much luck with lovers over the years."

"Better luck than me" laughed Alice but there was a serious side to her statement as she had been engaged five years ago but the man had suddenly broke it off for no apparent reason.

"You're better off without that bastard" growled Ella, "I always thought that he was only after your money anyway."

"Yeah, he must have been, he married someone richer than me didn't he."

"And that didn't work out either did it" replied Ella and both women laughed again.

"Yeah, the rat finally showed his true colours" said Alice with a hint of venom in her voice.

After a moments silence and a little more wine drinking, Ella plucked up the courage to tell all to Alice.

"How long have you known me Alice?" Ella suddenly asked.

"About twenty years now, why?"

"And I... have always been truthful to you haven't I?"

"Yes, about most things I guess."

"Well there is something I have always wanted to tell you..."

"You're... not a man are you?" interrupted Alice and both woman laughed out loud but Ella quickly became serious again.

"What is it Ella, c'mon spill the beans; I have always been here for you."

"You have and I will always love you for that but prepare yourself for what I am about to tell you and please do not freak out on me."

"I'll try not to" said Alice smiling but she was now really intrigued by what Ella was about to say.

"I... am not what I seem."

"What do you mean Ella?"

"I... am not human, well, I was human over three hundred years ago."

Alice went silent for a moment then she suddenly burst out laughing, "What's in that wine you brought here?" she quipped but she sensed that Ella was being serious, she could hear it in Ella's voice.

"I mean it Alice, feel my hands."

Ella stretched her hand toward Alice and then Alice carefully touched her hard marble-like skin; she did not pull her hand away though, she began to caress Ella's skin with the intimacy of a sculptor...

"Like stone... like marble" Alice gasped.

"Yes, it is a reaction to the sun, a protection; I have always been careful to never touch you when my hands were like that."

"You must be like a living statue... but how can that be, what are you?" asked Alice and this time there was a hint of panic in her voice.

"I am something called a Luxar... Charles is a Luxar, he saved me when I was a young girl; I was dying, he made me drink his blood..."

"What... like a fucking vampire!" exclaimed Alice as she stood up in shock, Ella was aware that she was trembling.

"Yes... no... I am not a vampire, the Luxar are similar but they are not of this world... they do drink blood but only animal blood. Charles came here to protect us from evil Luxar beings who are known as the Malos."

"My God... this is just so surreal!"

Alice seemed to be totally disorientated now, turning one way then the next.

"Sit down Alice, please, I am opening up my heart to you; please do not hate me."

Alice sat down and fumbled for her glass of wine, she was still shaking.

"I could never hate you Ella, you know that. I… always felt something whenever I touched you, your skin seemed different, so why have you decided to suddenly tell me this now?"

"Something… has happened to Charles I do not know exactly what but I suspect it has something to do with the recent murders."

"The body skins at the marina? That sounded gross!"

"Also, the young couple on Marsden beach."

"My Lord, the reporter did mention 'vampiric,' you don't drink human blood do you?"

"No, of course not, just animal blood like I said: we do not kill anything."

"But you're drinking wine, or are you just pretending to?"

"No, I do not pretend, I was human once remember, I can eat or drink anything."

"You won't drink Rocky's blood will you?"

This remark made Ella want to laugh but she had to focus on what she was there for, which was the safety of Alice.

"Of course not… you do believe all this don't you Alice?"

"Your skin does not lie Ella."

"Good, then I shall tell you the main reason why I am here now… I think Charles may have been possessed by something, I believe that he may be a threat to you because I foolishly mentioned you to him; I think that he now may use you to get to me."

"Dear God, you have left Moonlux Manor then?"

"I am 'hiding' at Vincent's house, I think Charles or whatever he is might not know about my feelings for Vincent, about our whirlwind romance… I want to protect you. Come with me to Starry Night."

"Jesus, Life is never dull when you are around Ella, that's for sure."

"That's the spirit girl."

"And Vincent, is he a vamp… Luxar too?"

"No, he wants to be and now I think that he may have to be to help protect us."

"Are you going to… 'transform' him or whatever you call it?"

"Not me, someone else but I will tell you who later when I speak to Vincent about it."

"He does not know what you intend to do then? Fuck me, I'm suddenly in a Hollywood movie!"

Alice laughed and drank more wine then once again she became serious, "And if you made me into a Luxar, would I have their eyes, would I be able to see?"

Ella pondered this, it was something she had considered for years.

"I… think you would be able to see but I am not sure, your senses would increase ten fold certainly; you would be stronger, faster and you would inherit my Luxar ability, the power to fly."

"You can fucking fly? Bite me, bite me now Ella!"

This time Ella did laugh.

"It is not like that Alice, actually it is simpler although I did have to drink Charles' blood but that was because of circumstances."

"But you said that someone else would transform Vincent?"

"Yes and there is a reason for that, the power of flight is not enough to defeat what Charles has become."

"Who is this person then?"

"I… think it is time to get Vincent away from his new fishing buddy, it is time to tell him what I have planned for him."

"And me, what about me?"

"There are Luxars who are known as The Elders, I cannot transform a human without their approval."

"So you have their approval for Vincent?"

"No… but it is a necessity at the moment. I cannot contact them, the Luxstone ring that Charles wears is the only way."

"And if you did make me into a Luxar?"

"Then the Elders might delete you."

"Damn, they sound like heartless bastards."

"They are wise and eternal, they have protected this realm for years and I cannot question their rules. Their reason would be that they do not know you, that you might be too easily influenced by the Malos."

"And?"

"And you might develop the taste for human blood."

"Oh yeah, I see now… but you will ask them?"

"We have to get through this first" and suddenly Ella called to Vincent, it was time to tell him what she had in store for him.

JENNA

Eventually the young girl that Vaag had abducted regained consciousness. Jenna Shaw's eyes drowsily flickered in the light that shone through the iron bars of the door's small window.

Jenna was disoriented, still in shock and still shaking. The small dark room that she was in was cold and damp, there was no furniture and she had been lying on the floor. She sat up and looked around, it was like a bad dream to her, a nightmare that seemed to be real. *Did I really see a moving living statue?* was one of her first thoughts then she thought, *Where is he... where am I?* and her next thought sent a cold chill through her young body, *What is he going to do to me?*

The light spilling in from the door window was a source of comfort though, Jenna stood up and peered nervously into the adjacent room. For some reason it was not what she was expecting; it seemed like a scientific laboratory from another age but not creepy like something in some old Frankenstein movie; it looked comfortable and well ordered with long wooden tables and padded chairs. One of the walls was covered in books and there was even a large fireplace in which a fire was burning sending a wave of welcome heat to Jenna's cheeks. This warmth helped soothe Jenna's rising panic and as she stood staring at the hypnotic dancing flames, a face suddenly appeared before her in the door window...

It was Richarde but his skin was no longer white.

"You are awake… good, good. I have made food for you."

"Fuck your food!" shouted Jenna, "What do you want from me, who the fuck are you?"

"You swear too much girl, but that will change."

Jenna had moved away from the door but she was transfixed by Richarde's face at the window, which was made to look even more sinister because of the iron bars in front of it.

"I am in the body of Charles Richarde and I am the god of both life and death, it will be up to you which one I am this day."

Jenna was trembling heavily now, "What… do you mean by that?"

"I mean that if you do what I say then you will live, it is as simple as that. You are to be a servant for my queen, we will both drink from you when we desire."

"No! No… you're fucking mad!" shouted Jenna and she then sought the darkness in one of the cell corners.

"I understand your fear… sorry, I do not know your name."

At first Jenna did not want to tell her captor her name and then she suddenly thought that if he knew her better he might be more reluctant to harm her; already her instinct to survive was kicking in.

"My… name is Jenna" she muttered feebly.

"Well now Jenna; if you eat your food, I will reward you."

"With what?"

Jenna was crying now.

"Next to this desolate cell is a large comfortable bedroom, one that Richarde used when steeped in his studies. Do as I say and the room will be yours."

"Who is this Richarde you mention?"

"Richarde is me, I am Richarde."

Richarde began to laugh.

"It must be hard for your young mind to understand my pretty. Now, do you want this food, I will let you eat it in the bedroom?"

Jenna suddenly became focussed and resolute, *If I agree, it will mean that he will open the door and maybe I can make a run for it,* "Okay Richarde… I will do as you say."

Richarde suddenly became angry, "You will not refer to me as just Richarde, my name is Charles Richarde but you will call me Master, understood? If you do not, I will kill you and drink all your blood!"

Jenna realised that the madman thought that he was some sort of a vampire, her mind had not yet come to terms with what she had seen when Vaag abducted her.

"I… understand master" replied Jenna and then she walked towards the cell door. A key turned in the lock and the door creaked open…

Suddenly Jenna pushed through the door into Richarde's laboratory, she looked quickly around for another doorway and saw a stone stairway in corner to the right of her that was obviously the way out… she ran towards the stairway and Richarde only laughed.

Richarde lifted his hand sending a gush of air that pushed Jenna to the wall next to her stairway to freedom.

"Naughty, naughty girl, but you do have spirit and I like that; however, you will need to be taught a lesson now!"

Richarde went to her and released his tight grip of air then he grabbed Jenna's arm and literally spun her back into the cell.

"You will now spend the night here again my pretty. In the morning I might let you have breakfast in the bedroom, if you behave yourself."

As Richarde closed the the cell door, Jenna slumped down against the cold stone wall. She began to sob and cry until eventually she fell asleep.

But it was a sleep full of nightmares…

Of white statues that moved

And vampires in evil laboratories

And in the distance

There was always a woman in a dark cloak with a large hood

Standing, waiting, smiling

With blood on her lips…

The Queen of Death.

JENNA'S DREAM

There was a sharp pin in her forearm…

But Jenna did not wake from her deep slumber

Jenna Shaw was exhausted

It felt as if she was floating

Drifting away to somewhere warmer

Soft and comfortable

On her naked skin

Above her the white statue

But his skin was not hard

Only his penis was hard

The white statue was smiling

As he slowly entered her

She tried to fight but it was no good

She was too weak

Then she thought that she heard children singing…

No good fighting with sticks and stones

Here comes Vaag

To drink your bones

"It is only a dream… a dream" Jenna murmured
But a cold pleasure surged through her
As her virgin blood flowed from her
She was worried about the bedsheets
But they were not her sheets
It was not her bed
And the grinning white statue
Licked her virgin blood
Suddenly he moved faster on her
In and out
Like a well oiled machine
That would never stop
Jenna wanted to be kissed
But the white statue was showing no expression
It was as if he was concentrating
In and out
Faster…
Until the sperm of the white statue
Entered her with the force of a fire hose
And her pleasure exploded
Joining with the sperm
As it flowed inside of her
Green sperm with sharp piranha teeth
Looking for eggs to eat
And the children were still singing…
We must behave
We must dance and play
Or Vaag will drink our bones
This day…
"Don't… don't… please!"
And the green sperm turned to white
And as Jenna's climax subsided
The white statue withdrew from her
And Jenna shuddered
She wanted more
She wanted the dream to continue…
And the white statue entered her again
Harder and more brutal this time
And this was what she wanted…
And when Jenna woke from her exhaustive sleep
Her body still tingled with desire
It vibrated with a new passion
As if it was suddenly older

Than her teenage years
And the smell of the room was different
She was no longer in the cold damp cell.

ELLA

Vincent returned with Rocky from his extra long chat with the river fisherman and sat down at the table with Ella and Alice. Ella had gone for another bottle of wine and refilled Vincent's glass. Vincent looked at the two friends and then asked, "You two had a chance to talk then?" and his gaze shifted to Ella.

"We certainly have" replied Alice.

"So you now know Ella's true background and the reason we are here today Alice?" asked Vincent.

"It… really is something to take in, I am still trying to get my head around it. But I am glad that Ella has finally opened up about it, I don't know how she has held something like that in for so long."

"Necessity Alice, if people knew what Charles and I really were, our lives would become a media circus."

"Or maybe it would be a freak show" interrupted Vincent suddenly, "The Amazing Vampire Woman and The Oldest Man in the World, roll up, roll up…"

The two women laughed at Vincent's flippant comment but they knew that there was some truth in it, what Charles and Ella really were had to remain a secret. Vincent then returned to the problem at hand, "So what do you plan to do Ella, you and Alice cannot hide from Charles forever?"

"Precisely" started Ella and she held Alice's hand tight, "Charles is much older than me which means that he is much stronger than me, there is no way I can defeat him head on… and there is no way I can contact the Luxar Elders for help because Charles has the Luxstone ring."

"But if you had an ally, if there was someone else with the same abilities, then it would be a case of two against one?" said Vincent eagerly and Ella knew what he was inferring.

"Not the same abilities" replied Ella, "Charles would still be too strong."

"How come?"

"Like I said, his age… the only way to defeat Charles is with Luxar Fire."

"What the devil is that?" interrupted Alice.

"It is a fire that can burn our hard marble skin. When Charles saved me, I inherited his abilities and special power of flight. Luxars have different abilities and are hereditary; that is how I can fly, because Charles' blood mixed with mine, the change in me was more or less spontaneous."

"But if you cannot contact the Elders then how will you gain this Luxar Fire?"

"Not me Vincent, I cannot alter my initial ability… I thought that you would be the one to accept the Power of Fire?"

Vincent stood up immediately, he could not believe what he was hearing…

"Me? It is what I have desired since I first met you… but what, I mean how is that possible since you do not possess such a power?"

"Sit down Vincent, calm yourself down and drink more wine; I am about to reveal another secret to you and Alice."

BULMER

Back at police headquarters, Bulmer and Davis had set up a special operations room and on a large white board they had started to pin up pictures of the victims and what they knew so far.

"I'll put the pictures of that poor couple on the board as soon as I print them off Bull" said Davis as he wrote a new heading on the board - MARSDEN, which was next to ROKER MARINA. All the pictures of the victims and known possible suspects were displayed on the board - Salty Laing, Cathy Rolf, the missing Alan Rolf, Janet Eastley and now the young couple was about to join them. Bulmer stared at the board for a moment then took the dry wipe pen from Davis and wrote a new section heading - VAAGA.

"You still intend on going to that island then Bull?"

"Aye… and I have a feeling it won't exactly be a jolly outing, that's for sure."

Davis shivered, "Exotic tropical islands appeal to me but not fucking cannibal ones. Glad you asked me to stay put here; I'll take my chances with the local vampires."

Bulmer laughed, "Things have got a little surreal around here Bob and that means we need to expect the unexpected."

"That has already happened Bull."

Bulmer laughed, "You're fucking right there man… okay, where's Cooky then?"

Detective Chief Superintendent Cook was Bulmer's immediate superior and head of the homicide department.

"It's Saturday man, where do you think he'll be?"

"The fucking golf course, that's where; I hope he's got his phone with him."

Davis laughed, " He has to have it with him, department rules man."

"Good, I hope I interrupt his fucking swing."

Bulmer phoned Cook and after a moment, Cook answered.

"Hi Bull, what's up? Tell me you have a lead."

"Sorry to disturb you sir, it is about the marina bodies and possibly the Marsden case."

"Go on."

Bulmer went silent for a moment, he realised that he had not thought it all through properly but that was him, a 'bull in a china shop' sometimes.

"I'm asking for your permission to go to the island of Vaaga."

"Isn't that the island that Rolf visited before they made their way home?"

Bulmer was surprised that Cook had remembered this fact that he had mentioned to him.

"That's right sir, I think Rolf's disappearance is key to this investigation now."

"And why is that?"

"I…"

And this was the bit that Bulmer had not quite rationalised properly yet.

"It's a gut feeling sir."

"Oh, one of DI Bulmer's famous gut feelings. You want to fly to…. where the fuck is this island again?"

"West of the Western Sahara and south of Tenerife sir."

"You want to fly to Western Sahara on a fucking hunch Bull? And anyway, isn't it owned by Western Sahara? it could take days to get official permission to set foot on it."

"I intend to fly to Tenerife sir, I have checked the island out, apparently Western Sahara does not own it, that was just a rumour; Vaaga belongs to nobodyas far as I can tell so I thought the Tenerife police could help me out with a helicopter?"

"Look Bull, what do you seriously hope to find on that island?"

"I… think that black body on the stone slab… is maybe Rolf's burnt body?"

"What?"

"I think it maybe the murderer who took that last picture on Rolf's camera."

"Fuck Bull… but seeing it for yourself, I don't see how that could help?"

"The scene of the crime sir and if it is Rolf's body then his family need to know this" Bulmer said bluntly and Cook instantly felt like an imbecile, Bulmer imagined Cook's embarrassed burning red cheeks lighting up the golf course.

"Yes of course Bull, you are right. Okay then, you have my approval, make your preparations. I only hope that the Tenerife police will help you out."

"If not, I can always hire a boat sir."

"Sure… good luck then Bull" said Cook but then he had to say one last thing, "But watch out for those fucking cannibals."

Cook's sarcastic laughter faded as Bulmer turned his phone off.

Funny fucker thought Bulmer but he was smiling because he was on his way, all he had to do now was contact the Tenerife police and book a place for his short stay.

ELLA

Ella decided that she would tell Vincent and Alice about her 'new secret' back at Starry Night, she still believed that it was the safest place to be. After helping Alice pack her essentials, the intrepid trio and Rocky headed back to Vincent's house near the village of Ryhope.

Starry Night was a pre-Victorian mansion, nowhere near as regal and imposing as Moonlux Manor but it was still a very impressive building. The Harper family had been landowners and farmers and over the years a great wealth had been acquired by them which had eventually been handed down to Vincent. This money had enabled Vincent to pursue his artistic dreams, it had not been an easy road though by any means, mental health issues had become a constant factor for Vincent but after the feedback of his recent exhibition, it seemed that his ambition had been finally realised. Vincent had a new obsession now though and Ella was about to reveal something concerning this, something that would both excite and change his life forever.

While Ella helped Alice unpack and settle into one of the large guest rooms, Vincent prepared an impromptu meal of baked pizzas, sausage rolls, pickles and a selection of sauces. When Ella and Alice joined Vincent in the dining room which looked out onto his conservatory studio, Vincent poured them both a glass of wine while he decided to have a pint of beer, he had decided on Newcastle Brown Ale as he sensed that he might need something stronger for what Ella was about to tell them.

"Well you are quite the resourceful host" quipped Ella when she saw the food that Vincent had prepared for them.

"Just stuff I had in… I don't eat pizzas all the time mind" Vincent replied and both Ella and Alice had to laugh.

"Well that's a relief" Ella had to say.

Alice had fed Rocky but he was sitting patiently for whatever pizza bits he could scrounge and that was when Killer the cat crept menacingly into the room.

"O oh" said Vincent, "Look who has returned, not sure if he is here to welcome Rocky though?"

Alice stroked Rocky on the head who was sitting faithfully beside her, "Rocky does not mind cats to my knowledge, I think he actually respects them."

"Killer's never been scared of dogs, I just hope that he does not see Rocky as a threat."

Suddenly there was a tense atmosphere in the room as Killer slowly weighed up Rocky staring intensely at the seated dog. Rocky just seemed intrigued by the one-eyed black cat that was obviously sussing him out. Rocky then decided to make the first moved and cautiously went slowly toward the cat, his tail wagging and his head held low.

"Vincent, I think you may have to get Killer out of the room" said a worried Ella.

"No, I think it will be alright, Killer would have attacked Rocky by now if he thought that Rocky was a threat."

Rocky's head was now facing Killer directly but the cat just purred and then rubbed his body against Rocky then scurried beneath the table.

"Phew, that was tense" Vincent breathed out with relief.

"And I think he wants pizza too" laughed Ella.

The cat and the dog seemed friendly which enabled the three friends to eat their food in peace and when they had all ate their fill, Rocky and Killer included, Ella knew that it was time to tell Vincent and Alice what her plan was.

"Okay, I have told you about how strong Charles is and how Luxar Fire is one of the things that may defeat him should he prove to have been compromised."

Vincent was really impressed by how Ella was sounding, she had really switched into Protector mode. Ella continued, "There is a way to acquire the Power of Fire…"

"And that is?" interrupted Vincent eagerly.

"In the Durham countryside there is a place called The New Sanctuary, a low-key Christian secret society that has existed since the ancient persecution of the Christians. The New Sanctuary are aware of the Luxar and have been for hundreds of years..."

"And one of them has the Power of Fire?" interrupted Vincent once again.

"Yes and no, if that makes sense?"

"No" and this time it was Alice who was puzzled.

"When a Luxar dies, they go through a process called Ascension."

"They go to Heaven?" asked Alice.

"Of that I am not sure, I really hope that they do, that we all have the same Saviour... what happens is that their body slowly turns to pure Luxar blood and this process, depending on the age of the Luxar can take hundreds of years. The bodies are usually kept in heavy glass coffins in a family crypt for this."

Vincent was thoughtful then he suddenly burst in, "You're telling us that this 'Sanctuary' has such a Luxar... in a bloody glass coffin!"

"Yes, you are right Vincent, she was the Protector before Charles."

"And now she is turning to blood... my dear Lord."

"If I am correct, her Ascension is close to completion now."

"Why did she not go back home to Terralux?" asked Alice quietly.

"I think she came to think of this reality as her home as I am sure Charles does, or at least the Charles that I know" said Ella and a red tear filled one of her eyes.

"And this lady had the Power of Fire?" asked Vincent who was aware that Ella was feeling a great sadness for what had happened to Charles, he knew that he had to get her to refocus again.

"The lady is called Lu'na and yes, her special ability was the formidable Power of Fire."

"But you said that you could not inherit any other ability?"

"That is right Vincent."

"So... you want me... to drink Lu'na's blood?"

Ella felt like laughing suddenly but she managed to suppress it.

"You do not have to drink the blood Vincent, it can be injected into your system, it should be able..."

"My God, I am to be a vampire at last!" shouted an exuberant Vincent as he stood up suddenly from the table then, "Wait a minute, what do you mean by should?

"A Luxar, not a vampire Vincent" Ella had to point out again, "Lu'na is dead but her Luxar blood still lives, it should be able to transform you. Are you willing to take that risk Vincent, even if the transformation does not work? I cannot see any adverse reactions occurring. Charles would know more about this than me but obviously that is not a current option."

A sudden sadness consumed Ella and again tears formed in her eyes, something she had been fighting to conceal since her suspicions about

Charles had arose. Vincent went and hugged Ella and Alice reached out and held her hand tightly.

"Dear.. Charles" Ella stuttered, "What in God's name as he become?"

"We cannot think about that, I think Charles would want you to do the right thing and that is the only thing that matters."

"You are right dear Vincent, it is something that Charles and I have discussed; the Malos must not prevail, no matter what the cost."

Vincent went for a bottle of brandy and poured out large glassfuls for everyone before sitting down again.

"So… when do I get Lu'na's blood then?"

"So you are willing to try this? It will mean that you will never be human again."

"Fine by me, lead me to her."

"I… need to speak with the head of the Sanctuary first, a delightful lady called Salome Wynter, I am sure that she will agree to this."

"And if she doesn't?" asked an anxious Vincent.

"Then I will cross that bridge when I come to it; there is no reason why she should be adverse to it, she would have probably wanted permission from the Luxar Elders but that is not possible of course now."

"What happened to Lu'na's ring then?"

"It was given to Charles before her Ascension."

"Of course, I should have realised. So when do we go to this Sanctuary?"

"Tomorrow is Sunday, still very much a holy day for the Sanctuary but I am sure that Miss Wynter will not mind us visiting given the circumstances."

Vincent raised his glass, "Here's to tomorrow then and the New Sanctuary… right lasses, this has all been a bit of a worry since we found out about the Malos and what may have happened to Charles, how about a bit of music to lift our spirits?"

Ella was proud of Vincent, she knew that he was trying to raise moral between the three of them but if Charles was indeed a Malos or whatever now then Ella knew that they were in for the fight of their lives. Vincent put The Black Keys 'Let's Rock' album on the cd player and Ella tried not to imagine what lay ahead for the three friends. No matter what happened to her, Ella was determined that no harm would come to Vincent and Alice.

JENNA

Jenna Shaw's eyes opened slowly like they did not want to open at all. There was a warm feeling between her legs which was possibly because of the strange erotic dream that she had experienced during the night and her head felt heavy and drowsy, almost as if she had consumed too much alcohol the night before. Jenna was only a teenager though and did not usually drink alcoholic drinks to excess but it definitely felt as though she had a hangover… then it came back to her suddenly like a rising sickness… but she was no longer in the cold bare stone cell, she was in a warm bed, her head on a soft pillow.

Jenna sat up suddenly and cast aside the thin black duvet, she was going to be sick. She jumped from the bed and saw that she seemed to be facing a small bathroom. Jenna ran to the toilet and threw up heavily into the bowl, she was disgusted to see that her sick was green and this made her vomit again… and then her body reminded her that she had not been to the toilet for some time. She sat on the seat and sobbed but she was also thankful that she was no longer in that desolate cell.

And then Jenna realised that she was naked and that meant… she flushed the toilet, quickly washed her hands then stepped back into the adjacent bedroom where she noticed that her clothes were neatly folded on the chair next to the bed.

"That… monster did this" Jenna exclaimed and a voice suddenly responded from the bedroom door that was now open…

"I am not a monster… well, not all the time."

It was Richarde and he began to laugh loudly at what he had just said. Jenna's hand instinctively covered her breasts then she grabbed her clothes and retreated quickly back into the bathroom. She had been wearing blue jeans and a white t-shirt with the words '*Believe*' on it in italics. Richarde was standing in the doorway now.

"Do not worry my dear girl, I will not look… I have seen what I wanted to see anyway, and very pretty you are too I may add."

More laughter.

With the bedroom door open, Jenna could smell the enticing odour of a cooked breakfast. Eventually and tentatively, Jenna stepped from the bedroom into the tower basement and saw that Richarde was sitting next to the fireplace to the left of the room, reading a book.

"I have not lit a fire my dear but the central heating, I think that is what you call it, is on. On the cooker to the right of you is a fried breakfast although it really is about lunchtime I think, do you normally sleep so late?"

"You can stuff your eggs up your arse you monster… what do you want from me?" Jenna shouted with all the venom she could muster.

"Ah, you have not lost your spirit, that is good. I have told you what I want from you; you are to be my maid, yes, that is the word, our handmaiden."

"Our?"

"Oh, you will meet my queen soon and I am sure that she will approve of my choice of servant."

"The fucking police will be looking for me now mister… and when they find me, you will be put away for forever!"

"Forever is a long time, but those bumbling cops, that's right isn't it, 'cops'? They will never find you because you will never leave here."

Silent tears rolled down Jenna's cheeks as Richarde stood up from his chair and carefully placed the book that he had been reading down onto the table that was in front of the fireplace.

"I think I will leave you now Jenna Shaw and let you settle into your new abode; my laboratory is fully self contained as you can see, I am sure that you will be happy with it for now."

"How… do you know my surname?" stuttered Jenna.

"Quite simple really, it was in your little purse that was in your so-called hoody."

This made Jenna feel sick again, she had not wanted the monster to know her full name.

Richarde walked across to the right hand corner of the room and the curved stairway.

"Eat the food dear Jenna and then relax, I myself am feeling quite hungry" but before Richarde disappeared up the stairs he had to add, "Oh, I am afraid that I had to take Richarde's portable computer and those little television buttons, I know that they would have given you access to the outside world."

When Richarde reached the top of the stairs, Jenna heard the click of a lock being turned. She knew that there was no other way out, that she was in a basement; then something odd struck her, *Why did he say Richarde's portable computer?*

LUNCH

Speaking to and smelling Jenna had made Vaag hungry, hungry for human blood. He went up to the top of the tower and removed Richarde's clothes. His naked body turned instantly to white as the glorious rays of the sun bathed him. Vaag had concluded that a naked body was better for hunting during the day, sunlight was reflected from the white skin causing a slight camouflage with the clouds behind him and a possible disorientating blinding glare for his prey, it also meant that a quick shower would remove any traces of blood, he would not have to worry about the possibility of Ella finding any blood-stained clothes due to the scent. And of course there was the simple fact that Vaag liked to be naked. Vaag's eyes scoured the surrounding countryside as they had when they had located Jenna, this time they spotted a solitary figure standing perilously close to the edge of a cliff. The figure was located south of the coastal village of Seaham and Vaag noted that there were no other humans near for miles.

Perfect day prey Vaag thought then he headed up amongst the clouds at great speed then southwards to the cliff edge.

The lonely figure was a woman who was standing as close to the edge of the cliff as possible, looking down to the jagged rocks and the heaving sea below that seemed to be calling to her. The woman was young, probably late twenties and she was sobbing and muttering to herself. Vaag could smell death all around her, the need for death, there was also the smell of alcohol and drugs.

"Why… why?" the woman repeated, oblivious to the presence of Vaag behind her…

"I can help you" Vaag said suddenly.

The woman spun around almost falling over the edge. She gasped out loud while her tear filled eyes tried to focus on the seemingly white statue that was standing naked in front of her.

"Are… you an angel?" the distressed woman managed to ask and she could not really believe that she had just said that.

"I am the angel of death, come to ease your suffering."

Suddenly the confused woman began to laugh hysterically, "I'm hallucinating, aren't I, that is why I am standing here talking to a bloody white statue? "

"This is no illusion, I am real, I am Vaag the Bone Drinker but it is not your bones I want this day, it is your blood."

"You're not an angel then.. you're a fucking imaginary vampire!"

The woman was scared now, scared by the cruel trick her mind was playing on her; so much so that trickles of urine dripped down her legs, the situation now seemed real and not some pathetic drama of self pity. The woman thought about running from the obviously imagined creature but she knew that she did not have the energy. She suddenly decided that she wanted to live, to face her demons head on…

Unfortunately she was facing a demon called Vaag.

"I can smell the fear running down your legs and that really appeals to me; look, you have made me erect but I do not have the time to fuck you because of the bloodlust."

Then Vaag sprang at the woman…

And they dived down from the cliff top together

Into and under the cold seawater below

Vaag bit at her like a starving wolf

Or maybe a heartless shark

Of course the horrified woman tried to scream

But the uncaring water consumed her voice

The bloodlust was upon Vaag

And he bit into every part of her salty body

Swallowing both her blood and the sea

The macabre feast did not take long

And Vaag propelled himself up and away

From the bloody wreckage of the dead woman…

Up amongst the cover of the clouds and back to Moonlux Manor and the comfort of a nice hot shower.

This was a new experience for Vaag; the woman had wanted to die and he had the pleasure of granting her wish, *These pitiful self destructive humans will provide a good constant source of food* he realised and this thought warmed his cold heart.

ELLA

Ella was the first to rise at Starry Night on Sunday morning, it had been a late night, the three friends doing their best to put the circumstances that they now found themselves in to the back of their minds. She cooked breakfast for Vincent and Alice but did not wake them, they could heat up the food whenever they were ready to eat it.

Ella was focussing on what lay ahead and that meant contacting Salome Wynter at The New Sanctuary. It was now mid-morning, Ella had wanted to phone Salome earlier but had decided that this would be a more appropriate time. Ella had both Salome's personal and Sanctuary number, she decided on her private number.

"Hello Ella, it has been some time I hope you are well?"

"It has been some time Salome and I hope that I am not disturbing your Sunday morning?"

"You know that you can phone me any time Ella, there is an important function here today at the Sanctuary but that does not start until noon. How can I help you?"

"I cannot explain fully on the phone but it concerns the recent gruesome events on the coast."

"I… saw that on the news and you can guess what I was thinking?"

"Malos."

"Correct, Charles knows that he has full support of the Sanctuary resources to call upon if it is indeed Malos connected."

"I would advise you to avoid any contact with Charles at the moment."

"What?"

"Like I said Salome, I need to see you to explain fully."

"Of course; will seven tonight be okay with you, I can cancel the function if you want me to?"

"No, seven will be fine what I have in mind concerns Lu'na."

"Now I am intrigued, you know Professor De Salle is responsible for the continuous vigil and observation of Lu'na's Ascension. Whatever you have in mind, I would prefer the professor to be there, he now resides here full time."

"Of course; I am glad that the professor will be there, his advice on this matter will be most welcome."

"So shall I expect you at seven then?"

"Yes, we will be there."

"We?"

"I think you will be in for a surprise Salome when you find out what I intend to do… but I do feel that it is a complete necessity."

THE NEW SANCTUARY

At 6.15pm, Ella and Vincent were in his expensive four seater pick-up and were about to go to The New Sanctuary in Durham. It was decided that Alice was to stay at Starry Night with Rocky and Killer and she wished Vincent "All the good luck in the world" with what would be the most important and dangerous thing that he had ever done.

Just as Vincent was about to start the car engine, Ella's mobile phone rang…

"It's Charles, what shall I do, ignore him or answer him?"

Vincent replied quickly, "Answer it, string him along, make him think that you do not suspect anything."

"Of course, you're right" replied Ella then she answered the call.

"Charles… I have been meaning to phone you, do you have any news concerning the Malos?"

Vaag had expected this, he had decided that it would suit him better if he were to never find the Malos, that way he could blame all his feeds on them.

"No dear Ella, unfortunately I have not, the Luxstone ring has not been able to detect them and that is unusual but not impossible."

Vaag quickly checked Richarde's memories, the ring was capable of detecting Malos but it was not 100% guaranteed that it would locate the creature.

"It is not certain that the ring will locate the Malos, you know that Ella."

"Yes, I know that the Malos are capable of evading the ring" conceded Ella but she was so sure that Richarde was lying, she immediately thought that he had not even bothered to go to Marsden beach.

"So when can I expect you back at Moonlux Manor? I have a wonderful surprise for you."

This so-called 'surprise' instantly chilled Ella and she did not want to think about it.

"I… have decided to stay with Alice for a few days, she is… not well."

"Oh… I am sorry to hear this" replied Vaag but there was no real sympathy in his voice, "So can I not expect you back here even for a short while?"

"No… no. I must stay with her until she is feeling much better, you know that she is blind so she will need a lot of help."

"She is blind?" was Vaag's sharp reply.

"Of course, you know that Charles?"

"Yes… of course I do, I am sorry. Well, your surprise will have to wait and I am sure that you will love it when you do return here."

"I… I am sure that I will Charles."

The phone call ended abruptly.

"What was that all about?" asked Vincent immediately.

"He says that he has some 'surprise' for me… and he was lying, lying about the Malos that he could not detect them. And he did not seem to know that Alice is blind, he has known that for over twenty years!"

"Conclusive proof then that he is not Charles. Do you think that he suspects that you realise the truth?"

"No, I think he does not and that is a good thing for now… but he will kill again, he has probably done that already."

"Then the quicker we go through with this and confront whatever he is, the better."

Ella's hand softly brushed Vincent's cheek, "Are you sure that you really want to go through with this my love?"

Vincent's face became stern and his eyes focussed with a look of steely determination.

"More than ever now, Charles is definitely not Charles, whatever he is needs to be eliminated before more human lives are lost!"

"It could be dangerous Vincent, the blood of Lu'na will be powerful. I do not think that her blood has been given to a human before, maybe in the ancient times but there is no record of it as far as I know."

"I'm willing to take the risk, it is what I have always wanted since I met you… and we need this power of Luxar Fire do we not?"

"Yes, I think we will need it" replied Ella and then she kissed Vincent warmly on the cheek.

"Right, let's rock 'n' roll then!" declared Vincent and as he started the engine the car stereo came on and the song STOP by the Black Rebel Motorcycle Club's blasted out of the speakers…

"Perfect" Vincent muttered as they screeched away from Starry Night.

JENNA

After Richarde had left the basement room, Jenna did realise that her stomach was empty, a weak sickly feeling that needed filling. She went to the cooker which was on the stairway wall, right of and next to two worktops and cupboards which in turn were next to a small fridge in the corner. In a frying pan on the white cooker were bacon and eggs, a slice of thick fresh bread which had been cut and placed on a large black plate next to a tin of beans. Jenna picked up a slice of the still warm bacon and began to chew it slowly and while she did she surveyed the basement.

The large room was square, to the left of her was the bedroom which was next to the two cold cells. Directly in front of her was a long table, the left side of the table was for eating Jenna assumed and the far right side had been where Richarde's laptop had been. Beyond this table was another table which had scientific specimens of the head in glass boxes - two eyes, an ear and a brain which made Jenna squirm somewhat. To the left of these boxes was a human skull with the areas of the brain mapped on it. On the end of the table to the right was a large leather bound notebook which was open and next to this book was an old fashioned fountain pen and ink well.

In the left hand corner was a full sized anatomy model, showing the insides of the human body, Jenna had seen something like this in the school science department but it was not as big. Next to this model were two large bookshelves which were full of antiquated books, some looking dusty and centuries old to Jenna but this did not interest her, what interested Jenna was above the fireplace.

On the right wall was a large tv screen but Jenna could see no remote controller on any of the tables but underneath all of the tables were a series of thin drawers. Jenna stuffed another rasher of bacon into her mouth and then proceeded to go through the drawers. When she came to the drawer that was next to the leather notebook, she found what she was looking for. But the controller in her hand did not look like any tv remote controller that she knew, it was square and metallic and it only had a few buttons - ON, OFF, OPEN, CLOSE, UP, DOWN.

"What the fuck's this then?" Jenna blurted out and as she pressed the ON button a green light on the side of the controller came on so she pressed the OPEN button… suddenly there was a faint whirring noise in front of her and to her great surprise, the two large bookshelves began to open… revealing what appeared to be a large wide lift.

"Of course, that is how they got all this furniture down here, this could be my way out of this fucking madhouse!"

Jenna ran into the lift and pressed UP on the controller which she just had to kiss when the lift began to move slowly upwards. Jenna felt a rush of adrenalin surge through her exhausted body providing a new source of energy as the wide lift came to the ground floor. Jenna pressed OPEN again and this time the opposite side of the lift opened revealing Richarde's recreational room.

Jenna cautiously scanned the room before stepping out of the lift, she was sweating nervously now and scared again but she knew that if she was careful she might be able to make her escape. Jenna put the lift controller into her back pocket and stepped into the large room, directly opposite her across the room was a door which she quickly ran to. The door opened into a wide hallway and to the right of her was a double doorway… *the front door!* thought Jenna and she went immediately to it. To her great disappointment the door was locked and there seemed to be no way it would open from the inside as there was no keyhole, *Damn, some sort of electronic security locking system, the bastard must be rich, she thought* Jenna assumed, *Surely there is a way out back?* So she ran down the hallway into the large banquet room…

"What the fuck is this place?" she said looking at the massive painted glass windows that dominated the walls then she saw the conservatory through the far door and sprinted to it, *Has to be my way out!* but once again the conservatory door was locked.

"Fuck... fuck, fuck it!" Jenna shouted in frustration then she picked up one of the chairs and smashed it as hard as she could against the glass door... but the chair broke and not the glass.

"What the?"

Jenna hit her hands hard against the glass but again it did not break, "Fuck... fuck!" Jenna shouted again.

Then suddenly a soft voice from behind called to her, "There is no need for such language my dear Jenna, the glass is reinforced and totally shatter-proof. I think Richarde had it installed to keep unwanted guests out... and now it keeps my guests inside, how ironic is that?"

Jenna turned to face Richarde, the late afternoon sun reflecting brightly off his white skin. He was smiling but it was the smile of a predator who knew that his prey could not escape. In his hand was a syringe.

"I can see how upset and disappointed you are so I thought a mild sedative might help you relax."

Jenna instinctively turned to the conservatory door trying in vain to once again open it but Richarde was on her in an instant, administering the sharp needle to her upper arm... Richarde then took her to the large comfortable settee and and sat down with her.

"Sit with me, I want to talk with you, there is no need to be alarmed."

Richarde's voice was soft and gentle, almost hypnotic, the seasoned voice of a psychiatrist, "Let the serum do it's work and I will tell you who I really am. I will like that and I think that you should know now."

Jenna felt like she was floating suddenly but she did feel relaxed, like she had no energy, her body was limp and there was no frustration and fear of the white statue man that she was sitting next to.

Richarde began...

"I think you may have realised by now and I am sure that I given it away that I am not Charles Richarde, my name is Vaag and I have existed for thousands of years.

Jenna thought that she was hallucinating now, that it was all a dream, *Did he say thousands of years?*

"I can know that you will find that hard to believe, to comprehend even but I can assure you that it is true. I was 'born' on what I know now to be a strange large meteorite, something that had come from the stars themselves. My parents were gods and I was their gift to this planet. At first I had no form, no definite shape, I moved like lava across my mother rock, feeding on any bacteria and insects I could find. Then as I grew there were larger animals, snakes, small reptiles and then mice and rat-like rodents that I would inject my green acid into so that I could drink their bones and everything else that was inside of them. I took their form and evolved with the evolution of the island I was on, to monkey. And as a monkey I watched the first strange men arrive on my island in crude canoes, and they tried to eat me but I ate them. The men in canoes stayed on my island, and they eventually brought their women and started to worship me because when I drank their bones, I became them; they even wanted me to feed upon them which became a sort of a spiritual ritual for them and me."

Jenna pulled away from Vaag, even in her sedated state, these were horrify images for her as she imagined…

A black moving shape
Like a living slime
Consuming snakes and rats
And monkeys
Then the monkey
Inserting the horrible green acid
Into the primitive man
Into the mouth and the anus
And then the monkey became the man
The man feeding on other men
Then woman that screamed
As they turned to green liquid
As Vaag drank them dry
Bones and all…

Vaag brushed his white hard fingers through Jenna's hair, he could see that she was sweating, see the horror and revulsion in her eyes.

"Do not fret my little Jenna, I ate to live like any other species, like any other creature on this world and when I did I became them; I looked exactly like them and I inherited all of their memories, memories that did disturb me sometimes and when they did, I simply fed again and became someone else. It was an addiction but it was also a necessity, I did what I did to survive.

And I evolved with my people, they worshipped me as a god, they ate each other and I ate them. I was known as Vaag the Sharib Aleizam, the Bone Drinker. My name is Vaag because of the sound of the people as I ate them, and the sound of me enjoying them as a meal. And the children sung songs about me…

No use fighting with sticks and stones
Here comes Vaag to drink your bones
And
We must behave
We must dance and play
Or Vaag will drink your bones this day…

Then my people became great and feared seafarers, capturing and eating whoever they came into contact with. And eventually I travelled the world with them; experienced new civilizations, some far more advanced than my people... but I always went back to my island and my 'rock from the stars' because it was where I came into being, where I was born, where I was a god... but an unhappy god at times because in all of my travels, I never found another of my kind."

Suddenly Vaag looked sad, he picked up the empty syringe and gently pressed the needle into Jenna's wrist, she tried to move away but she could not.

"Do not worry my dear, a little drink to soothe my sadness, I will take no more; I do not want you to be weak, I want you to be strong for my queen."

Vaag filled the syringe with Jenna's blood then placed the needle into his mouth and sucked at it like a baby with a milk bottle.

"Aah, that's better... shall I continue now? I can see that you are wondering how I came to be here, how I came to be the human Charles Richarde, the lord of Moonlux Mannor in this cold country called England. It is both simple and complicated and involves the Devil Himself, the one known as Lucifer."

Jenna's weary eyes widened suddenly in disbelief, she began to move her head from side to side. In her mind, a horned creature with a goat's face and wide serpent's wings was moving above her, then moving inside of her, it's long snakelike tongue licking her, "No, no" Jenna mumbled but Vaag continued...

"I can see that you are distressed by this but I want you to know what happened, it is because of Lucifer that I am sitting with you this day."

Jenna wanted to scream but she could not.

LUCIFER

"I shall start this like a story and I will be as brief as I can, the effects of your sedative will be wearing off soon and I want you back in your room, safe and warm for the evening, I may even give you the television buttons. So let me continue...

One day, my people brought me a beautiful princess to eat, she was called Lanar and she was from the rich small country of Annon which was north of Egypt then but this is not a history lesson this is a lesson about the power of love. At first I did not want to consume Lanar, she was so beautiful that I wanted her to be my queen... but she did not want that, she instantly hated me, hated my island and my people. She said that her warriors would find her and her husband to be too so reluctantly I drank her bones and I became her.

And her future husband did find me but there no was no army with him. He was alone and his name was Lucifer.

My people were scared of him. He arrived as a black winged demon and tore through my village and my guards like they were nothing. I was in my temple, at my altar that I had carved from the meteorite that had gave me life. My people were praying to me as usual when Lucifer burst in.

Suddenly the demon stopped and he reverted to human form, it was as if this great beast was now vulnerable and shaking, I could see tears in his eyes as he came slowly toward me…

"Lanar, Lanar my love… I thought I would be too late but I am here now, to take you away from this evil and damned place."

I tried to trick him because I sensed immediately that he was stronger than me. I wanted to be him, I knew that this was a being of great power and combined with my might I would become invincible.

"Take me to my bed-chambers first, I need your body now, then we can leave here" I said to Lucifer but I had foolishly forgot that I had consumed Lanar on my black glittering altar… and her thin withered brown skin was still there, an offering to my celestial altar and a reminder to my people of my great power. I knew that I did not have time to remove it and as Lucifer kissed me, I saw the reflection of her dead face in his eyes…

"What… how can this be!" he shouted in shock as he pulled away from me, revolted by what he was looking at… my extended mouth surged towards Lucifer's lips, my green acid within me bubbling with lust, ready to fill him in a instant…

"You are not Lanar, you are from the pits of Hell, what sort of twisted creature are you?" cried out Lucifer in disgust.

My mouth returned to my face, her beautiful face…

"We can be one, we can be together forever" I said seductively and I did mean it but the look on Lucifer's was one of sudden anger.

"No!" screamed Lucifer looking at what was left of his beloved Lanar. He then turned back into his true demonic form and I tried to flee, I was powerful but I knew that I was not as strong as this imposing creature before me.

He grabbed me with the speed of a cheetah…
And threw me onto my altar
Beside the skin of his Lanar
Which seemed to enrage him even more…
I tried to fight but it was hopeless
I was in the grip of the Devil
My mouth and sharp teeth
Tried to piece his skin
So that my green acid could consume him
But his skin was as hard as stone…

He then grabbed one of the altar's oil lamps and set fire to me, the flames licked at him too but there was no pain for him, I now realised that he had been severely burnt at some point in the past and that is why he looked the way he did, the black and charred creature from Hell.

My people fled from the temple as I slowly burned, Lucifer's black arms keeping me pinned to the altar as the hungry flames began to consume me. In his red eyes I could tears again as he watched the remains of his beloved Lanar ignite beside me.

"Lanar... Lanar, my love, my love, forgive me please" I heard him say through the sound of the fire. And through the hungry flames before my sight faded, I could see Lucifer as he watched his Lanar become ash... it was the sight of a demon in utter despair...

Lucifer then went on a bloody rampage of hatred and revenge; destroying my village and my people, old men, old women and children too...

Then when he was satisfied that all was dead, he flew away from my island; I could hear the beating and crackling of his strange wings as they took to the air and I can still hear his anguished cries and screams to this day. My pain as my death approached increased and the temple began to darken around me as my life began to fade like a dying candle... Lucifer thought that I had died and I guess in some ways I did.

But the flames died out, leaving small burnt parts of my flesh and a heart that was still beating... and there I was, in that thin black flesh, lying on that altar, some days conscious, some days not and always in constant excruciating pain, and in my pain my hatred of Lucifer grew, almost keeping me alive I realise now, the need for revenge one day as he had exacted revenge on me... and once again I slowly began to feed on the insects that came to feed on me, on scorpions and rats, on any creature that tried to eat me and over the years my body started to take some sort of shape again but like Lucifer, I was black and burnt, my eyes began to form again and slowly there was some sort of vision but I still could not move. I was a black motionless form with muscles that were disconnected and in complete disarray. I was a helpless body that had almost lost the will to live as I lay on my stone altar and waited, trying to regain my strength...

And one day a man called Alan Rolf entered my temple, an explorer from this part of the world; he was a photographer from these shores and the memory of movement returned, inspired by the chance of human food...

And that is how I came to be here.

This is the story of Vaag the Bone Drinker, the One of Many Faces.

And why you should worship me as your god."

Jenna's face was emotionless, like she had just heard some new dark fairy tale by the Grimm brothers that she just could not believe.

"I know that is a lot for you to take in Jenna, a lot for someone as young as you to comprehend so I will take you back to your rooms now and let you think about what you have just heard. Charles Richarde is hungry again and I am tempted to drink from you again but I will not."

Vaag gently lifted Jenna into his arms and removed the lift controller from her pocket. He then took her to the lift and then down to the basement and the bedroom and laid her on the bed; he was tempted to have sex with her, to make her feel loved and to satisfy his desire once again but he resisted the temptation, he was feeling compassion for Jenna and this was new emotional territory for Vaag and he did not know why he was experiencing such feelings for her.

Back in Richarde's recreational room, Vaag thought further about Jenna and why he was so concerned about her and the only thing he could conclude was that somehow a residue of Charles Richarde's emotions was influencing him but he was not too worried about this, it was something he would monitor he decided and he was even interested to see how his feelings of Jenna would develop now.

Vaag then became bored by his unusual situation with Jenna and thought about Ella and the fact that she had not yet returned from going to see the woman called Alice. When he rang Ella, she was about to leave with Vincent to go to The New Sanctuary.

VINCENT

The New Sanctuary was situated in a secluded area of the Durham countryside. The original New Sanctuary had originated in ancient Rome during the time of the Christian persecutions and was the first secret safe haven for Christians. Over the years it remained secret but became powerful and prosperous. There were now New Sanctuary's all over the world and the one in Durham was nearly as old as the original Sanctuary in Rome. One of the largest and richest Sanctuary's was the one in White Palms California but the Durham Sanctuary was renowned for it's expertise in historical and paranormal studies. As Vincent and Ella approached the large double gates which displayed the words *YOUR SINS ARE FORGIVEN,* the gates automatically opened for them.

There was a long wide drive to the main building, a drive that was covered on both sides by tall trees. Once they reached the New Sanctuary building, it seemed to Vincent to be an elongated mansion that had been added onto an old church which was to the right of it. Vincent noticed that part of the building just before the church jutted out from the circular part of the building that was the connection to the church. On top of this circular segment was an enormous glass dome that seemed to be divided into eight panels.

At this extended part of the building was a wide circular driveway that obviously surrounded the whole building. Vincent turned left on this circular drive and when they stopped at the end of the building, Vincent noticed that there was another extension on the left hand side of the building like the one that they had just drove past. Vincent realised that the entire building was in the shape of a large cross. The car was now parked at the bottom of this 'cross' which was obviously the main entrance. Looking from the car, Vincent saw that above the wide double glass doors was a large silver cross beneath which were capital letters spelling out THE NEW SANCTUARY ENGLAND. Vincent sat staring at this then said dryly, "This must be the place then?"

As Ella and Vincent stepped out of the car, Salome Wynter was waiting to greet them. She was dressed casually in a white blouse and tight black trousers, it was obvious that the function that she had been involved with was now finished.

Ella was wearing a thin Puma sports hoody and after entering the building, Ella lowered the hood.

"It is good to see you again Ella but if only it had been under different circumstances" said Salome as the three of them walked down the long corridor to the centre of the Sanctuary, "I will take you directly to Professor De Salle's quarters which is located behind the nearby campus library. The glass coffin of Lu'na is kept in the crypt directly below this building."

Professor De Salle's quarters was in fact an old building that looked like it had been built in the middle ages and looked like a small mansion now, Vincent guessed that the crypt had existed first. Professor De Salle was waiting at it's old arched doorway.

"Hello again Ella, you look as young as ever" said the professor and he shook her hand and gently kissed her on the cheek. Jon De Salle and Salome Wynter were two of only a few people in the Sanctuary who knew the truth about Lu'na's glass coffin. There was a French accent to De Salle's speech which Vincent thought was probably Belgium Wallon. The professor was in his early seventies and there was definitely an aura of academic distinction about him. He was wearing a light herringbone jacket but his blue shirt collar was open, there was no formal tie. De Salle's hair was now completely grey and combed back and Vincent immediately realised that the professor reminded him of the distinguished British actor Peter Cushing that had appeared in many of the Hammer retro horror movies that Vincent loved so much.

How apt thought Vincent and he felt like chuckling but he did not.

After De Salle was introduced to Vincent, he invited everybody inside. He then took them through a series of rooms, each room resembling a small library until they came to a room which De Salle called his study which was basically a large recreational room. Vincent noted that that there were considerably less books in this room but he did think that the books that were there were probably De Salle's favourites.

In front of a black ornate fireplace there was an old wooden coffee table surrounded by three padded leather chairs and a matching leather sofa. Ella sat on the sofa and Vincent, Salome and the professor sat on the chairs. Salome and De Salle were seated in front of the professor's work desk and Vincent was seated next to Ella and on the wall behind them was an extra large, life size mirror which stretched down to the floor.

Alice through the looking glass? thought Vincent, *Am I about to enter Wonderland?* And this thought made Vincent smile.

"Can I get anybody a drink before we start?" asked De Salle but Salome stood up, "I will do that professor, you carry on, G&T's everybody?"

They all nodded eagerly. Then De Salle spoke to Ella directly, "Now then Ella, I believe you are here because it involves the lady in the glass coffin?"

"I am indeed professor" replied Ella as she took her drink from Salome, "And I will get straight to the point I think that Charles has been compromised."

"Compromised?" interrupted De Salle.

"I… believe that he may have been consumed by the Malos or indeed something else!"

The professor looked thoughtful for a moment then he said, "This concerns the victims at the Marsden beach, yes?"

"Yes, and also I think the horrific events at the Sunderland marina."

"Have you ever come across anything like this in your studies professor?" Ella asked anxiously.

Once again the professor became thoughtful and this time his face appeared to darken. Then he suddenly stood up and went for a large leather bound book that was on his study table. He flicked through it nervously until he came to the pages he wanted.

"Actually, there is something recorded by Lucifer Heylel now that I think about it."

"What?" gulped Vincent, "Did you just say Lucifer?" but De Salle appeared to ignore Vincent's question.

"This is an account taken from the city of Meccus Royal Records, from the now mythical ancient Mediterranean country of Annon which sadly no longer exists now, one of those old small rich countries which did not survive the test of time, swallowed up eventually by the Egyptian expansion thousands of years ago."

"What book is that?" Ella had to ask.

"It is my book Ella, A Paranormal History Volume One. This volume is more concerned with the factual, in Volume Two, I focus more on my personal opinions and experiences."

"And you say that this is an account by Lucifer Heylel?"

"Yes, as far as I can gather he was a very successful architect at the time and eventually he became engaged to the Annon princess known as Lanar. Unfortunately this princess was captured and abducted by the Vaagen, a seafaring tribe of cannibals that were greatly feared around those times. Apparently, Lucifer Heylel set off in search of his princess and somehow eventually found her and…"

"And what?" interrupted Ella.

"And it appears she was not what she seemed."

"What do you mean by that?"

"Well, by Heylel's account, Lanar had been taken to the Vaagen king who was revered as a god by his people - Sharib Aleizam, The Bone Drinker, The One of Many Faces. According to Heylel, he thought that he had saved his beloved Lanar then he saw the remains of Lanar's empty withered skin on the temple's 'green' altar."

"So, Lanar… was somebody else then?" asked Ella and she could feel her heart beating louder.

"My God, the skins at the marina!" gasped Vincent as De Salle continued…

"The royal account concludes with Heylel destroying the Bone Drinker by flame but unfortunately Lanar's remains were also burnt, caught up accidentally in the rage of Lucifer, so her remains sadly never returned to Annon. It appears that Lucifer was inconsolable in his grief and Lucifer Heylel is never mentioned or heard of again in the court of Meccus."

It was Salome Wynter who spoke next, "So let me get this straight Jon, you are saying that this cannibal king drank people's bones and then became them?"

"It… would seem so, 'The One of Many Faces' would seem to suggest this."

"Who is this Bone Drinker?" asked Ella.

"His name is Vaag."

"But didn't you say that Heylel destroyed him?" asked Vincent.

"By Heylel's account he does… but maybe Vaag survived somehow?, Heylel said that he burnt and destroyed both Vaag and his people with the 'Fire of Revenge' but maybe he did not check that Vaag was indeed dead?"

This revelation sent a cold chill through all the people in the room.

"So… it could be that we are not dealing with Malos then?" Vincent mused.

"I fear not now" said Ella, "I… think that those people at the marina may have somehow come across this Vaag, an immortal creature stranded on his empty island."

"The boat owner Rolf, he is reported as missing but no 'cannibal island' is mentioned in any report that I saw" added Vincent.

"The police might have wanted to keep such information to themselves?" suggested Salome.

"Then maybe the victim's did find this island and maybe The One of Many Faces became them?" Vincent continued

"And somehow this creature called Vaag came across Charles?" Ella interjected, "This could mean that we are now facing someone who is as powerful as the Bone Drinker and a Luxar!"

"If it is then he was someone who was nearly destroyed by fire so perhaps it will be fire again that will finally destroy him" declared Vincent.

Ella reached into the inside pocket of her jacket and pulled out a large syringe then looked at De Salle, "What Vincent is basically saying professor is the reason why we are here, we need La'na's Power of Fire, we need her blood as Vincent wants to become a Luxar. This amount of blood will be enough to complete the transformation."

"A noble act young Vincent, I admire your courage and commitment."

" I think that it is time to go to 'The Lady in the Glass Coffin' then" said Salome and she walked towards the large glass mirror on the wall.

"Through the looking glass then?" Vincent had to say.

"Correct" replied Salome and she touched the side of the mirror causing it to slide open, "Come with me then, Lu'na awaits you."

Salome stepped through the opening first causing a series of lights to automatically come on.

They were in a short hallway that led to a set of wide steps that went down to a large circular area. Here everything seemed to be cobbled stone but the ground had been cemented over and painted white. There were six arched open doorways and Salome went to the one straight ahead of the stairway.

"Lu'na's room is this way."

Soon they were all in a large white room in which there were two modern looking steel chairs and a glass table on which there was a large vase with two white orchids inside. Against the far wall on a table covered in a decorated white linen sheet which draped down to the floor was Lu'na's glass coffin. The coffin was oblong and inside, Lu'na's red bones seemed to be floating in her blood.

As Salome, De Salle, Ella and Vincent surrounded the glass coffin, they saw to their dismay that the front of Lu'na's skull had eroded completely.

"I know it looks grotesque but it is the Luxar Ascension" said De Salle.

"Her… bones are red" gasped Vincent.

"They are turning to blood Vincent" said Ella, "Blood that can be passed on… and it will be this night."

De Salle pressed a hidden button on the side of the coffin and the glass hinges automatically opened the lid.

"Before I draw Lu'na's blood into this syringe" said Ella, "you must be aware that the transformation may be dangerous Vincent."

"We have discussed this Ella, this is what I want."

"I wanted Salome and Professor De Salle to hear that."

Ella dipped the needle of the syringe into the sparkling blood and filled the syringe to capacity then put it back into her inside pocket.

"Now Ella, have you decided where to complete the transformation?" asked Salome. Ella looked at Vincent whose face was blank.

"I suggest that you do it here at the Sanctuary, we have adequate facilities should there be any problems."

"We intended to go back to Starry Night but what you say makes sense, thank you."

"Good, come with me then to the Sanctuary hospital area."

"Hospital?" blurted out Vincent nervously and Salome smiled, "I am sure that everything will be fine Vincent, it is just a precaution, you are in safe hands here" and Salome looked toward Ella confidently.

From Lu'na's room, they continued along the tunnel until they came to another set of stairs.

"The hospital is above us and a new life awaits you there Vincent" Salome said enthusiastically.

The hospital room was not what Vincent was expecting, it was more 'homely' almost like they were in someone's bedroom.

"Are you sure that nobody lives here?" asked Vincent and again Salome smiled.

"Not for some time Vincent."

"Sit on the bed Vincent and hold out your arm" said Ella. Salome and De Salle stood behind her.

"Have you done this sort of thing before?" asked Vincent who did sound nervous.

"I have helped Charles on occasion in the hospital and I am a trained nurse but no, I have obviously never done this before."

Vincent smiled, "I could not be in better hands, let's do this. "

"You will feel the rich powerful blood of Lu'na surge through your system, merging with your blood, changing you, you must be strong… you will probably feel drowsy, do not fight it, sleep if you have to, let the blood transform you."

Then Ella gently inserted the needle into Vincent's arm and injected the blood of La'na, "Let it flow through you, let the blood of a Luxar become you."

When the syringe was empty, Ella withdrew it and placed on the bedside table then held Vincent's hand tightly.

Suddenly Vincent's eyes became bloodshot…

And his body began to shake

Then his skin went pale

Then white

Vincent felt two of his teeth tighten

As if some invisible dentist

Was sharpening them with a fine chisel…

"I… feel fine" he said almost comically

Then he dropped back onto the bed

As if he had been kicked by a wild white stallion.

VINCENT'S DREAM

Vincent's mind was suddenly bombarded by a multitude of images…

It was as if he was travelling back in time in an instant

Tumbling back until he came to a place that was white and bright

So white and bright that he could hardly see

His eyes fought hard to focus, to see…

The hazy naked form before him

A woman lying on a wide bed

Gentle breezes flowing softly around her

Her skin was white and her eyes were red

She reached out to Vincent

And her mouth opened

Showing her small sharp teeth

That sparkled like marble in the brightness…

"Come to me" the woman whispered

Her voice unearthly, ethereal and erotic

"Drink my blood"

Vincent felt heavy suddenly

Like he had turned to stone

Like he was a statue

But slowly his legs moved

Driven by desire

As he walked to the white goddess on the bed

"I am Lu'na" she purred like a cat

About to lick the cream

Her voice was soft and alluring…

"I will make love to you, we will be as one"
Vincent's hand was shaking as he reached out and touched Lu'na
And her skin was soft not hard
Lu'na then placed her arms around Vincent's neck
And pulled him gently onto the soft bed
It was like Vincent was in a dream
An erotic dream that felt warm and wet
A hidden sculptor carving their desire
Two white marble statues
That had been inspired by love and the need for sex
And he was moving
Thrusting with his heavy might
Inside Lu'na
Lost in the woman's desire to live again
"I will be as one with you" she whispered
"Come now and join with me"
Suddenly Vincent exploded inside of her
And it seemed that the hot room was now full of sparkling stars
That had descended from the heavens to be with them
To surround and bless them with their celestial light
But as Vincent withdrew from Lu'na
Her white skin became red
As it turned to blood
Blood that dripped from the bed to the marble floor
Suddenly Lu'na's blood soaked lips
Were kissing Vincent
Her tongue inside like a red snake
Searching for and licking his very soul…
"Drink my blood now, if you want to live with me"
She said with an erotic urgency
A vampiric urge overcame Vincent
And he bit deep into Lu'na's throat
Sucking her blood as if he were a wild animal
And her body slowly became blood
And he drank and drank and drank
Until Lu'na was no more
Until the white sheet of the bed was completely red
And as he lay back
Full of the blood of Lu'na
His body began to burn
"No… no!" he cried
As the heat consumed him
like a living beast from Hell was inside of him…

"It is only fire my love, the Luxar fire is yours now"
Said Lu'na's voice inside his head
But the unbearable heat increased
Until Vincent could stand it no longer
Until the flaming heat surged through his body
Like some devilish demon that was trying to escape from him
And he began to burn
Began to scream
As he became a living human torch
The heat and pain too much to bear
And he began to pray
To any god that would listen
And the last thing he saw
Was the white face of Lu'na
Smiling…

***

It was not until noon on Monday that Vincent's eyes opened, fully bloodshot and sore looking. Ella knew that his red eyes were not the result of direct sunlight, it was purely because of the transformation. Ella was seated next to Vincent's bed and was wiping his brow with a cold damp cloth.

"Vincent" she whispered softly, "I have been waiting for you to open your eyes."

Vincent's head turned to the right but it was only Lu'na that he could see. She was dressed in a flowing white Roman gown and from the wide open doorway he could see the glowing ancient city of Rome that sparkled before his eyes like precious marble.

"Lu'na, is that Rome I see?"

"I am not Lu'na Vincent, it is I Ella; you must concentrate, you must come back to me… or you will be lost to me forever."

"Not… Lu'na?"

Vincent was confused.

And still his body burned.

The day was hot and the city of Rome was sweltering and shimmering in the distance, the heat haze rising in front of the white buildings causing them to blur and move.

"I will survive this fever Lu'na, I will live for you."

"Yes, live my dear… live for me."

Ella then kissed Vincent softly on the lips and for a moment he seemed to remember her, Ella thought that she could see it in his eyes. Then he drifted off back to sleep again.

And slowly the city of Rome became the city of Sunderland and he was back again in Starry Night.

VAAG

After his phone conversation with Ella, Vaag was angry, "Who is this blind woman that keeps my queen from me? I must kill her, eat her, drink her bones!" he shouted like a spoilt little boy having a tantrum.

Vaag stormed around the room then removed his clothes.

"I will eat, I will drink this night!"

Then from the door to the rear gardens, Vaag took flight in the brightness of the moonlight. He flew high and fast, the wind surrounding him like a living shield as he glided through the night… and as he scoured the land below he was like a nocturnal owl looking for prey until he came to a deep river and a lonely bridge.

And on that bridge there was a young man who had climbed over the side railing and was now peering into the dark water below him, only his shaking hands held him from the death he sought below.

Vaag hovered over the man like a patient deadly hawk and listened to his relentless sobbing…

Pathetic human, he deserves to die and what an honour it will be for him to die by my hand or indeed by my teeth and this humorous thought made Vaag laugh out loud.

"Wha... who's there?" the young man suddenly asked and it was obvious to Vaag that like the woman on the cliff, this man had drunk too many alcoholic drinks.

"Someone who is very hungry" Vaag said coldly and the young man's sweaty hands slipped from their grip causing him to plummet towards the black water below. Vaag swooped down at great speed and pulled the man back up into the air.

"I do not want a wet supper this night" Vaag called out and the man's head turned to face Vaag.

"Are you saving me?"

"No... I am going to eat you, you are my Sunday night takeaway."

This remark made Vaag roar with laughter but only filled the man with total confusion.

What the fuck is happening? was the young man's final thought.

BULMER

Detective Bulmer had managed to book a flight with Jet2 on the Monday leaving at twenty to four in the afternoon from Newcastle Airport and arriving at half eight at the Tenerife South Airport.

Bulmer was travelling light, one suitcase and a backpack and he did take his tablet which had all his case notes for the recent investigations typed up on it; he knew that the flight back would be an opportunity to record any details of his trip to the Canary Islands. Bulmer really had no idea of what he was likely to find but he had to satisfy his 'gut' feeling.

By nine thirty Bulmer had checked into the Palms Tenerife Hotel which was not far from the airport. After Bulmer had unpacked his suitcase, he headed for the main hotel bar, he had never been much of a travel person so he was definitely in need of a drink.

Bulmer's girlfriend Susie had always bought his holiday clothes which he had hastily packed for his short trip and he found himself in a palm tree patterned short sleeved beach shirt as he headed downstairs to the bar.

Seated at the bar, Bulmer supped on a cold beer and a tall gin and tonic chaser. The room was only sparsely populated with people enjoying the vintage tunes played by a piano player who was dressed in a white tuxedo and a black bow-tie. Bulmer guessed that the hotel mainly catered for people like him, people on short stays but then he thought that maybe he was wrong with that initial assumption as after he had finished his drinks the bar seemed to fill up and a glamorous female singer joined the piano player dressed like a thirties starlet.

Play it again Sam Bulmer immediately thought even though he knew that the line was never said in the movie Casablanca, *or maybe it was, fuck it, I can't remember.*

Bulmer was suddenly aware that a Humphrey Bogart mojo had immediately overcome him which was heightened when the singer began to sing As Time Goes By.

Bulmer laughed to himself and ordered another gin and tonic with ice and while the barman served him, his mobile phone rang.

"Has to be Susie" he muttered to himself but when he looked at who was calling him he was surprised that it was the forensics doctor.

"Hi Bull, Bob told me where you are, I hope that the flight will be worth it… and I hope that I'm not troubling you at this late hour?"

"No, of course not Doc what ya got for me?"

"I've emailed what I could find on those similar unsolved cases to you."

"Thanks for that."

"But I can tell you what you really want to know now if you want?"

"Sure, hit me."

"Well, there were more murders than I thought and I was wrong about the most recent which was in 2011 on the Scottish border…"

"And…"

"And there were other cases, 2001, the nineties, the eighties…"

"A lot more than you initially thought then Doc?"

"For sure but there is one similar factor with all these murders…"

And that is ?" interrupted Bulmer.

"That there is a long time span between them all."

"Which probably means that they could not have been done by the same person?"

"That is right Bull, they go back too far."

"The mystery deepens then."

"It sure does, I thought that I would tell you this in person as it might save you some time?"

"I appreciate it Doc and yes, it will save me time… I think we treat this investigation as new and not part of a serial killer op."

"Could it be a copycat killer then?"

"I doubt it, don't you?"

"Definitely, I think a lot of those past cases have been hushed up anyway for some reason."

"Well thanks again Doc but I will look at what you have sent me."

"Cheers Bull, enjoy your short stay if you can."

"I will try" laughed Bulmer and the phone call ended.

Bulmer sipped his cool drink, he doubted that he would bother trawling through what the forensics doctor had sent him, he had to concentrate on what he and his partner Davis knew, *Tomorrow a Tenerife police helicopter will take me to the island of Vaaga and God knows what I will find there but tonight I will enjoy being Humphrey Bogart, maybe Susie will surprise me by walking into the bar so that I can say the immortal line, "Of all the gin joints in the world, you had to walk into mine."*

Bulmer listened to the singer, drank more gin and tried to forget about Vaaga.

***

Even though Bulmer had possibly indulged in his Bogart fantasy a little too much and had drank more than his fill, he was up early the next day, showered and ready for his helicopter ride which was scheduled for ten thirty am.

Bulmer's head thumped slightly like an annoying hammer in the distance and the heat was already uncomfortable but by ten o'clock he had eaten an extra large fried breakfast and was ready and waiting for the police car that was to be his taxi. Because of the heat, Bulmer had decided on a white sort sleeved shirt, khaki jungle shorts with heavy beige desert boots. In his backpack was his phone which Bulmer would use mainly as a digital camera, this was no way a tourist trip though and in some ways Bulmer wished that it was all over and he was back relaxing in the hotel bar, drinking a cool beer.

The police car was punctual and this impressed Bulmer as he had to admit that he did have the unfair assumption that the police in hot countries were a little laid back. Within minutes he was standing at the heli-pad which was attached to the airport, looking at the 'chopper' he was about to board. It was not long before the pilot approached him from the staff building a short distance away.

"Hiya, my name is Ramos, the guy who is gonna take you to that cannibal island" the pilot said shaking Bulmer's hand with gusto.

The police pilot was tall, well tanned with short curly black hair and a broad gleaming smile.

Bulmer took to him immediately as the pilot added, "Although I am not sure why you want to go there?"

"Hi, call me Bull, everyone else does, but no bull fighting jokes okay?"

Ramos' smile increased.

"Sure Bull, no problemo, let's get this bird into the air."

The island of Vaaga was about 186 miles south west of Tenerife and Ramos told Bulmer that "The flight would take about an hour, maybe an hour and a half."

"Cool" replied Bulmer who was now hooked up to Ramos with earphones and a microphone.

Their initial conversation was very basic, where exactly was Bulmer from, what was the place and people like?

"You have never been to Sunderland or Newcastle then?" asked Bulmer.

"No never, although I do know that one or two people from that area have enjoyed a stay in our cells."

Bulmer roared with laughter at this, "I'm sure they have, the sun tends to go to our heads and we end up drinking too much" he replied thinking shortly about how much alcohol he had consumed in the hotel bar.

The two policemen talked a little more then Ramos did get a little serious.

"Okay then Bull my friend, just why are we going to Vaaga?"

Bulmer opened up to Ramos, describing what had happened back in Sunderland and why he was on that chopper with him. Ramos was astounded by what he heard but he understood the reasoning of Bulmer, "So you think that you might find a body there?"

"Yes, I do… possibly, this case is so fucking weird man, anything is possible."

"Y'know my friend, I am the only one who volunteered to take you to this island…"

"What?"

"Three other guys turned it down."

"Can they actually do that?"

"Our superior gave us an option."

"So he thinks… what, that the island still has fucking cannibals living on it?"

"Who knows, I brought my gun just in case" replied Ramos and this time he roared with laughter.

"You're winding me up aren't you?"

Ramos stopped laughing.

"No my friend, I just like to be prepared, that is all."

"Amen to that bud."

And as soon as Bulmer had said those words, the island of Vaaga came into view.

"Wow, it is much bigger than I imagined" declared Bulmer.

"Do you have a specific area in mind?" asked Ramos as they flew closer to the island.

Bulmer checked his phone for Rolf's photographs.

"Yes I do; look for the remains of ancient jetty's, just eroded wooden poles in the sea basically."

Suddenly Ramos pointed down to the island.

"Down there Bull?"

"Aye, that looks like it man, cool."

"And wide beaches too with the tide going out, the helicopter will be secure... how long do you intend to stay here Bull?"

"Not long Ramos; Rolf's photographic trail leads to a overgrown stone temple, I don't think it is that far from the beach."

"And this temple you mentioned to me?"

"I think once I have been there and checked it out, my mission here is over; there is no way I can check this whole island out... and anyway, that is where Rolf's photographs end."

"A dead end then?"

Bulmer shuddered, "It might well be that."

Ramos put the helicopter down as close as he could to the opening to the jungle that Rolf had photographed.

"This is it, I'm sure of it, we're spot on Ramos" said Bulmer as he stepped down from the helicopter, "You gonna stay here with your chopper?"

Ramos laughed.

"I think my chopper is fine Bull, how many cannibals will be capable of flying it... no. I'm coming with you, this whole thing really intrigues me."

"Class, well my friend let's go... I can tell you now that as we near this temple of cannibals, you will find human remains, ancient bones on sticks but this is the guy we're looking for."

Bulmer showed Ramos a photograph of Rolf.

"I guess we have to hope that we don't find him?"

"Yeah, I suppose you're right... but if we did, it would solve one mystery."

Bulmer and Ramos hurried through the wide jungle path, scouring both sides for any sign of Rolf and soon they had come to a clearing in the overgrown village and the large temple.

"This is it bud, the place where they probably served human flesh for dinner, wanna take a look inside?"

"Not really my friend but let's do it."

As they neared the temple doorway, Bulmer noticed something that he had not noticed on Rolf's photographs, "Wow, never saw this on the pictures."

Bulmer's hand gently rubbed the small stones set in the walls of the temple, each stone had a different crude face carved into it."

"The faces of the villagers that lived here?" mused Ramsos.

"Maybe… or maybe the faces of the people that were on the menu."

Ramos shivered at this thought as he looked at the skulls that were still on the poles that surrounded the temple. Bulmer took photographs of the stone faces then reached into his backpack for a large torch.

"C'mon then Indiana Jones, let's get this over with."

Inside, the temple was dark, light only breaking through the open square windows at the top. Bulmer shone his torch down to the far end of the temple to where the altar was but there was no black body on it which was what he was expecting.

"That was where the burnt body was, on that altar."

"Burnt body?"

"I will show you the picture later."

Bulmer then shone the light of the torch to both sides of the temple, again he noticed a multitude of small stone faces.

"Nothing… but faces" muttered Bulmer then he focussed the beam of light closer to where they were standing in the doorway. To the right of them, Ramos thought that he saw something.

"There Bull!"

"What!?"

"Shine the light in the corner…"

"Fucking Hell man, it… looks like… skin!"

The two men walked cautiously to the corner where to their utter disgust and revulsion, Bulmer's torch revealed the remains of small human skin parts and even a hand, flattened in the dirt of the ground.

"Dear Lord God Almighty!" shouted Ramos, "A hand, but only the skin!"

Bulmer scattered the beam of his torch light, his adrenalin was now pumping through his middle-aged body at an alarming rate… and deep in the corner he found what he was looking for, "Oh no Ramos… look, it's the face of Rolf, or what's left of it!"

Ramos felt like being sick but Bulmer had seen this back home, the face and hand was detached from what was left of the body. Bulmer knew that most of the skin had been eaten by animals and insects. He reached into his backpack and pulled out a pair of surgical gloves which he put on his hands before taking photographs of the remains with his phone.

"I… gotta take this back with us bud, hold my bag will ya."

Bulmer was shaking slightly as he picked up the hand and face of Rolf and placed it in his backpack.

"I'll get a bag for this when I get back to the hotel" he said then he did cough up some green stomach bile that seemed to contain some of his breakfast.

"Are we finished here then my friend" said Ramos with his hand on Bulmer's shoulder.

"Yes, I think we are bud, let's get off this Hell hole as quick as we can."

On the journey back, both men consumed a lot of water as they tried to get the grisly sight of Rolf's face from their minds.

"So you think that whoever murdered Rolf is doing the same back in Sunderland Bull?"

"So you think it is murder then Ramos?"

"I think he has been eaten Bull" Ramos replied bluntly.

"So you think that our suspect is some sort of cannibal then?"

"I… think that he is some sort of… creature."

This statement by Ramos chilled Bulmer instantly and made him think, *How would a cannibalistic creature know how to operate a modern yacht, why would he want to go to Sunderland, there were much nearer islands, such as Tenerife?*

Bulmer's mind was churning… *And if I announce that I have found Rolf's remains, will that alert what we are looking for?*

This was a conundrum for Bulmer that needed serious thought and a serious drink.

***

After saying goodbye to Ramos, Bulmer promised that he would keep in touch and notify him of any developments. In return, Ramos promised Bulmer that he would not tell anyone what they had found on the cannibal island, he would even tell his superior that he had remained on the helicopter and anyway as far as Ramos was concerned, it was an English investigation and one that only concerned Bulmer.

Back at the hotel and after his backpack was safely in his room, Bulmer went straight to the bar to try and think logically about the new evidence that he had found. After three or four drinks he came up with an unbelievable conclusion…

The fucking thing becomes them
That's why they ended up in Sunderland
That's why Laing and Rolf's wife's skins were found
You're fucking mad man…
The heat has got to you.

Bulmer drank more and more, his mind constantly rejecting what he was thinking until he made the final decision to only reveal what he had found to his partner Davis and to get his opinion. Once this decision had been made, Bulmer thought that he could relax and look forward to the returning flight to Newcastle even though he had the face and hand of a dead man in his backpack.

VINCENT

Ella had decided to take Vincent back home to Starry Night, she thought that he needed familiar surroundings to ease him out of the grip of Lu'na's memories. Salome Wynter and Professor De Salle had agreed that this was a wise decision and Salome had organised a Sanctuary ambulance to transport Vincent back home. When Vincent awoke, it was late in the afternoon and he was in his own bed with Ella sitting patiently beside him… his head turned toward her.

"Ella, I'm home?"

"Yes Vincent, you have come back to me."

"I… have come back?"

"From Lu'na."

Vincent closed his eyes and tried to remember, Lu'na in the Roman gown, making love to her then Rome burning…

"Why do I have images of ancient Rome in my head?"

"Lu'na came through the portal to old Rome, then she came here to replace a Northern Protector who had been destroyed by a Malos."

"And she remained here until her Ascension?"

"Yes, and was then replaced by Charles; my worry was that her fire was destroying you but you seem calmer now."

"I… feel weak but much stronger, if that makes sense?" replied Vincent and he sat up on the bed as if he were in pain.

"Yes it does Vincent, the transformation is instantaneous, I think that not every human could survive it. You have done well to accept the Luxar blood of someone as old as Lu'na."

Ella was holding Vincent's hands tight and she noticed that his initial bloodshot eyes had gone now and this was a good sign she thought.

"My senses; my eyes, my ears, if I concentrate I can see the smallest things, hear things outside, people talking…"

"Your senses have heightened Vincent, it will take time for you to get used to them."

"I don't have any x-ray vision though" joked Vincent and Ella laughed then had to point out, "No, you're not quite Superman but when you feel stronger we will discuss whether you have received Lu'na's special ability."

Vincent looked at his hands and stretched out his fingers, "I… can… feel it inside, it's like a living flame wanting to be released from within me."

"We will discuss this later when you are feeling better and have fully rested."

"I feel fine now, even hungry."

"You have not eaten for some time my love, what can I get you?"

"Blood."

VAAG

Vaag had killed his latest victim on the grounds of Moonlux Manor. He had then dumped the body far out at sea, he reasoned that if the remains of his meal was washed back up on shore then it would just be another mystery for those two stupid policemen inspectors.

Before sleeping, Vaag had decided to watch television in Richarde's bedroom. The large screen was mounted on the wall facing the bed and all Vaag had to do was master the remote controller which he did easily by accessing Richarde's memories. To his delight he came across a series on one of the channels; it was called Hannibal and he enjoyed it immensely, he ended up watching four episodes before finally falling asleep.

When Vaag eventually woke up on the Monday morning, the first thing he thought about was Hannibal. Doctor Lecter had inspired him; he thought that it would be a nice way to enjoy a meal, to entertain it first, seduce it even, then have fun eating it. It seemed a very civilised way of doing things *and after all, I am very much a civilised man now*. Vaag even thought about buying a large incinerator for the waste disposal and he was sure that his future queen Ella would approve of this idea.

Vaag was in a good positive mood then when he jumped out of bed, the blood he had consumed during the night had been most enjoyable, filling him with a renewed positive energy. He even decided that he would return the tv controller for the basement television which he had taken away because he did not want Jenna to watch the screen on the wall. *She will like that* he thought and he suddenly realised that he did want her to be happy, he did not want a sour faced depressed servant and he did intend to have sex with her again so it was important that she was happy. Vaag even went to Ella's room with a large bag and filled it with clothes and undergarments that looked unworn and other things that women needed.

***

After he had showered and had cleaned his bloodstained teeth, Vaag took the television remote controller and the clothes bag down to the tower basement, only to find a despondent Jenna Shaw lying sideways on her bed, her pillow damp from tears.

"I thought I might find you eating or reading perhaps, there is a great selection of books here for you to study."

"Go away creep, I do not feel like eating or reading."

"So my little bird is sad then?"

Jenna sat up and looked at Vaag and his bag.

"I'm not a fucking bird, I'm a human being… someone you have kidnapped for your own perverted satisfaction."

Vaag thought for a moment then he asked, "What is a 'creep'?"

"Look it up on 'Richarde's' laptop… creep."

"Ah, so you have remembered my story then?"

"Some of it; some fucking fairytale you told me while I was drugged up… and what fucking drugs are you on?"

"I have never taken human 'drugs' as you put it, although I may try a few now that I know about them. I am sure that they will be like the hallucinatory concoctions my people used to drink and smoke."

"Yeah, knock yourself out with them, hopefully they will kill you!"

"I am too strong for any man-made substance to kill me, I am not human remember?"

A chill surged through Jenna, she could not really believe that Vaag was not human; he was just a twisted, demented pervert with a 'thing' for young girls, *He has not sexually assaulted me yet though, that was only a dream wasn't it?* thought Jenna hopefully.

Vaag stepped into the room and Jenna moved back on the bed.

"You still fear me then? That is good, that is what I would expect from a servant… but I do like my personal maids to be happy; look I have brought you fresh clothes, clothes that my queen has not worn, you seem a similar size."

"I'm not wearing any stranger's clothes, what do you think I am?"

"You will… and I will even wash the clothes that you are wearing now for you. Do you have any idea what that means? Vaag washing your clothes for you, I have never ever done such a thing!"

"And I bet you'll like it, pervert!"

"What is a 'pervert'?"

Jenna had to laugh sarcastically, *Maybe this madman is from another time and place?*

"Well then, I can see that my presence still 'irritates' you so I will leave my gift bag here… oh, and I do have another gift for you, you will find the television buttons in the bag also."

Jenna looked up and Vaag noticed the change in her countenance, it seemed like his decision to let her view the television had been a good one.

"I will speak with you later then my Jenna and hopefully you will be in a more positive mood."

Vaag turned and silently left the basement, leaving Jenna sitting staring at the bag. She thought that it might be some sort of a sick wind-up by Vaag but she did think that he sounded sincere.

After a moment of contemplating this she went to the large bag and emptied it onto the bed. She was surprised by the choice and quality of the clothes that were inside, they were very expensive and very stylish; t-shirts, dresses, blouses, tights, black trousers and jeans, all with designer labels, even the pretty and sexy underwear and Vaag had been right, they all did look new. There was even a make-up bag and an assortment of perfumes and sprays. And the thing she was looking for was there too, the remote controller or 'buttons' as Vaag had called them.

Jenna went straight into the main room and turned on the television screen that was on the wall above the fireplace. She immediately found the BBC news channel and sat in the large chair that Vaag had sat in, and watched and waited; she was hoping for news about a police search for her.

Time passed anxiously for Jenna and there was no report about her, she then thought that she would have to wait until the late local news on BBC One then suddenly the female presenter announced breaking news that at first Jenna did not think was about her, a video that had been recorded between two friends was being shown, a bright grainy reflection that seemed to show a figure that was completely white, then Jenna heard her name…

"In connection with the North East abduction of the teenager Jenna Shaw, this strange video image of a moving 'white statue' has been released on social media by Jenna's friend who says that this was the moment that Jenna was abducted…"

Jenna dropped the remote controller and sat back stunned in the chair; she was pleased that the police were aware that she had been taken and that they obviously must be looking intensely for her now but… *That white thing was Vaag… He killed poor Benny, squashed him like bug and I remember being lifted into the air now before losing consciousness, Vaag really is not human! He really is the monster from his fairytale!*

Jenna went into a state of shock, staring at the news but not hearing it, thinking about her poor dog Benny and how he had died beneath the foot of Vaag…

Then suddenly something dawned on her, without thinking about it too much, she realised that she had to do everything that Vaag asked her to do; she had to be good, polite and no swearing, she had to do nothing that would make him angry with her, she would even let him wash her clothes if he wanted to.

Jenna had to survive, she had to believe that someone would eventually find her, maybe his 'queen' even, whoever she was, *maybe this person would take pity on me and let Vaag's 'little bird' fly free?*

Jenna knew that she had to do everything that she could to please Vaag, she did not want to be killed by this real monster or even eaten by it. Tears flowed down Jenna's young cheeks because she had to forget Benny for now, because now there was the slightest feeling of hope, she had some sort of a plan.

VINCENT

"I… do… need blood" Vincent repeated but his words were broken and weak. He tried to stand up from his bed but his mind was too dizzy and he had to sit back down.

"Not yet my love, when you are stronger, when the transformation is fully complete. Lie back down now and rest, sleep through the night and I will get blood for you."

"But I thirst so much for it, it is like a bloodlust and I am scared what I might do."

"You will do nothing to harm anyone Vincent, it is not in your nature, that is why I could trust you with this gift."

Vincent lay back on the bed and his heavy head sunk into the soft pillow.

"Tomorrow then…"

"Yes my love, tomorrow you will become a true Luxar."

Sleep was instant for Vincent and Ella kissed him lovingly on the cheek before she went downstairs to speak to Alice who had been waiting anxiously for news of the 'reborn' Vincent.

Rocky was curled in his dog bed that Alice had brought with her for him and lying next to Rocky but not in his bed was a content Killer.

"Well the animals don't seem worried too much about poor Vincent" joked Ella and Alice smiled but she had to ask, "How is he Ella?"

"He wants blood" was her simple reply.

"Yuk!" said Alice in disgust and then she had to ask, "And how do you propose to get it for him, I'm not much of a blood donor and neither is Rocky."

Rocky's ears pricked up at the mention of his name and Ella laughed.

"Nobody's blood will be used, the answer is simple really; tonight I will take a large vet's syringe into the fields and fill containers with the blood of cows, the animals will not be harmed and they will not feel a thing. Initially Vincent will crave blood but then he will become accustomed to human food again, like I did, the process will take a few weeks though."

"So I better keep my neck covered up then?" joked Alice.

Ella laughed, "Yes, we do not want to tempt Count Vincent do we?" she said in a mock Transylvanian accent and both women laughed so loud it disturbed Rocky who just had to get out of his bed to see what all the commotion was about.

"I like that, Count Vincent, it sounds sort of cool" added Alice but Ella became serious again.

"Tomorrow, Vincent will be stronger; after he has consumed the blood, we will know if he can control the 'fire' or not?"

"And that is really important isn't it?" added Alice.

"Important? It is everything, without the Luxar Fire of Lu'na we are surely outmatched."

VAAG

Vaag was once again disappointed by the response of Jenna to his offerings but then he tried to put himself into her shoes, *Yes, I suppose that I would not be too happy about being forced to become a servant even if it was for someone as powerful as Sharib Aleizam. Still I hope her attitude will change because if it does not then there will be no alternative….*

Vaag's thoughts were becoming too depressive for him, he knew that he needed something to divert his attention. Vaag decided for some reason, to look through Richarde's diary maybe it was time for him to start socialising again. He was confident that he had accessed all of Richarde's memories now; that indeed, it would be hard for someone who knew Richarde to detect the presence of Vaag within him.

Richarde's diary was actually in his bedroom, on the side table next to the bed. Vaag skipped through the dates and the notes until he came to the current Monday.

"Ah, tonight there is a Pyschology Lecture at the Ramside Hall, perfect. I will dress for the occasion and attend, Richarde will be noticed again so there will be no chance that people will start thinking of him as a recluse."

The lecture started at 7.30pm and the Ramside Hall was not too far away from Moonlux Manor; it was on the A690, one of the many motorways that headed toward Durham City. Vaag took Richarde's classic German Mercedes from the seventies which was in excellent condition.

Vaag smiled, "This is some wheeled chariot and Richarde's choice of music is most excellent too" he said as Wagner's Ride of the Valkyries boomed out of the car stereo.

The Ramside Hall was as Vaag expected and indeed, Richarde had many memories of the hotel stored away in his memory banks. However, Vaag found the whole lecture boring and it was a chore for him to give the impression that the lecture was interesting throughout but at the end of the lecture as the various doctors and physicians made their way out out of the seminar room, someone did recognise Richarde.

"Hello there Charles, it is good to see you and I see that you have not lost your sense of style, the spotted bow-tie is exquisite with the white tuxedo, you sort of remind me of Bogart" laughed a man who seemed to be in his mid seventies.

"Yes... yes, I like to keep up my appearance; one has to keep up his standards, even in retirement."

"You have retired, that is quite sudden isn't it? What are you doing here then, just keeping in the social loop?"

Vaag quickly accessed Richarde's memory again and came to the face and name he required.

"Yes, you could put it like that and you Doctor Milan, are you retired now?"

"Me... oh no such luck, I have too many financial commitments, we do not all have something as lucrative as Moonlux Manor to fall back on."

"Indeed, I... am quite lucky in that respect."

"Well old bean, great chatting with you again but someone is waiting for me. Maybe we can meet up sometime, have a chat about things?"

"Yes, I would like that..." *And what a nice meal you will be too.*

Vaag did not feel like going straight back to Moonlux Manor, the night was still young and the Ramside Hall did have a late bar. Vaag took a seat at the bar and ordered a large double vodka with ice. Sitting there, he noticed that some people from the lecture were sitting drinking near him but none that were recognisable to Richarde's memory. However, sitting only a few seats away from him at the corner of the bar was a woman in a short tight fitting red dress, the woman had silver curly hair and seemed to be of a similar age to Richarde. When she ordered another drink, Vaag noticed that she was looking at him, he also noticed that she had an accent he had only heard on the television.

"I'm sorry… your accent?" Vaag suddenly blurted out and he half expected the woman to ignore him but she simply smiled and replied, "American… well, Boston actually."

Vaag quickly looked up America and Boston in Richarde's mind.

"Ah, east America?"

"That's right, here for the lecture actually."

"What, all that way just for that?"

The woman laughed, "Yes, I was a little disappointed, I came across it by accident and I thought, *you know what, I have never been to the north of England.*

"So… are you here by yourself then?"

"Yeah, I'm a psychiatrist, I tend to do crazy things now and then. I did notice you in the lecture hall."

"Yes, I couldn't wait for it to end."

The woman laughed.

"You don't look like a quack, you look like some heartbroken millionaire from a Hollywood forties movie."

Again the woman laughed.

"Quack?" Vaag had to ask.

"American for doctor; you look the same age as me, thought you'd know that?"

"Oh yes, sorry."

"Hey, why don't you join me, we can talk about the mysteries of the mind of maybe we can just get sloshed and have a good time?"

Vaag smiled, he liked this woman, she reminded him of Janet Eastley in some ways, he thought that she would make an interesting meal.

As Vaag took up a seat next to the woman he had to ask, "What does sloshed mean?" and once again the woman had to laugh.

"I'm going to enjoy tonight" she said then offered Vaag her hand, "I'm Annette Stephens and who sir do I have the pleasure of conversing with?"

"I am Va… Doctor Charles Richarde" Vaag replied and realised he was so close to telling Stephens his real name.

"Well, Charles, here's to you and me for surviving that lecture." Annette raised her glass and Vaag did the same with a devilish glint in his eye.

The two strangers got on like a 'house on fire' which were Annette Stephens words…

And the next thing Vaag knew, he was in bed with her, pumping hard within her until she quickly came…

"You're so big Charles… I've never felt anybody this big or hard before, I have to come to Durham more often" Annette purred afterwards and then the woman from Boston began to laugh which made Vaag laugh too.

But now Vaag felt hungry…

He felt like biting her all over her body

Cutting into her with his sharp lethal teeth

And drinking from her until she was completely bloodless

The American woman would not laugh at that

Then Vaag thought…

No, I will enjoy this woman tomorrow, at Moonlux Manor; in the style of Doctor Lecter maybe?

As they lay naked on the hotel bed, Vaag asked Annette, "How would you like dinner tomorrow night at my manor?"

Annette sat up, her large breasts and long nipples touching the sheets below them, "You have a bloody manor house? I knew you were fucking rich!" and she laughed again.

"You do not sound like a doctor when you are in this mood Annette."

"I'm an uncouth American remember? And yes, that would be so cool to have dinner at your manor."

"Good… the menu will be a surprise just for you."

"I like surprises" Annette said and her hand reached for Vaag's limp penis which immediately became hard and erect again.

"Man, are you even human?" Annette gasped as Vaag entered her again.

"Some say that I am not."

MOONLUX MANOR

While Stephens slept, Vaag left the Ramside Hall to return to Moonlux Manor. After having sex with Stephens for the third time, Vaag had arranged to meet up with her in Durham City at six pm the next day, he did not want the Ramside Hall to have video footage of her getting into his car, he could have sent a taxi he thought but the driver would remember the address if questioned by the police later. Vaag told Stephens that he had business in Durham City and Stephens that it was cool, that she could see more of the city then meet up with him. Vaag had been careful to choose a shopping mall with a basement car-park and the venue was an indoor cafe with no direct sunlight.

***

After a few hours sleep, Vaag woke up refreshed and looked out at a bright sunny morning. After washing he decided to go and see Jenna to see how she was and to his great surprise he was greeted by a 'new'

Jenna who was dressed in a lively flower-patterned mini-dress. Vaag then noticed something that he had never seen before, Jenna was actually smiling.

"Hello master, I have been expecting you. I have fried steak and made coffee for you."

For once, Vaag was speechless and a wide smile beamed suddenly across his face.

"It seems that you have come to your senses then sweet Jenna?"

"Yes, I think I have master. My role now is to serve you."

Vaag was slightly suspicious by this turnaround by Jenna but he was really enjoying seeing and hearing her like this.

"Good… good, my queen will be so pleased."

"And when will I get to meet the queen?"

Vaag frowned, "She… she is attending to a friend who is sick, I know not when she will return at the moment."

"She… sounds nice… and caring" and suddenly the look on Jenna's face become sad.

"Yes, I suppose she is nice and I am sure that she will like you. Now, shall we eat together?"

Vaag sat at the table near the cooker and Jenna served him the cooked steak, trying to smile all the time while she sat next to him.

After his meal, Vaag sipped his coffee, "That was quite delicious and you were intelligent to realise that I like my meat served very rare."

Then Vaag seemed to think for a moment, "Maybe, just maybe, you could cook something for me tonight, maybe the same dish because I am entertaining a guest this evening."

"That… would be… fantastic" lied Jenna who was really not expecting to hear such a thing.

"And you will have access to the main kitchen upstairs but not access to devices with wi-fi, no phones or laptops and of course, all the windows and doors will be locked securely, just in case you are tempted…"

"I… will be honoured… is your guest the queen?"

"No, someone I was with last night, someone I just have to eat."

Suddenly an icy chill swept through Jenna and tears formed in her eyes, "Please master Vaag, please do not let me witness this!"

Vaag felt a sudden unusual compassion for his young slave, "No, of course not, it will be an intimate night between me and my guest. Once you have served dinner you will go back down to your basement, I will lock the door after my meal."

"Of course my master" said Jenna bowing her head as the cold shiver continued to crawl slowly through her young body.

"Now, I will leave you to ponder the menu, let me know what you need and I will order an immediate delivery for you."

"But how can I let you know, I have no phone?"

"Of course you do not and we both know the reason why."

Vaag then reached into one of his pockets and pulled out a small intercom device.

"I came across this in Richarde's study, I think they were probably for him and my queen or maybe he used them for his work?"

"Walkie-talkies?"

"Yes, I think you call them that. I know children use them but these seem more expensive and sophisticated... and don't think that you can access the outside with them, I have checked them and they only communicate with each other. Good, here take it, call me when you are ready to."

"Yes... I will."

And after Vaag left Jenna, that cold feeling of anxiety and fear turned into an icy dread, *He is going to kill someone tonight...*

And bloody images of horror

Began to surge through Jenna's mind

It was as if her imagination was enjoying the chance to taunt her

Images of vampires

Of cannibal zombies

Feasting on the dead victim

On the dining table

Blood mixed with the dinner she had cooked

And Vaag smiling like Gary Oldman's Dracula

Coming towards Jenna like he was floating

Like he was on roller skates

With white ancient hands

Fingernails like long sharp claws

But then the shadow of Dracula evaporated

Like a wisp of smoke in Jenna's mind

And she was safe

Unharmed and alive...

But then...

At least it is not me.

She thought with relief.

Jenna's mental state of mind was changing, had changed...

The only thing she thought of now was *survival.*

STEPHENS

While Vaag was waiting for Annette Stephens at the small Durham mall cafe, he watched the multitude of bustling shoppers pass by him. He was sitting at a small table outside of the cafe and he marvelled at the array of different people and their different shapes and sizes and fashion senses, *there is a great selection of food here in this part of the world, different bones, different bloods* he thought then he realised that he had not had the urge to consume anybody totally yet, to fill their bodies with green acid and become them. *Yes, this Luxar body of Charles Richarde is simply perfect, just the right combination, there will be different ways of drinking their bones and I look forward to experimenting with this human herd.*

Annette Stephens was slightly late and when she arrived she had two large shopping bags with her. She kissed Vaag gently on the cheek.

"I'm sorry that I am a little late Charles, I just had to buy a few souvenirs."

"You are only late by ten minutes late Annette which is nothing in the eternity of time, I was enjoying watching the 'herd' pass me by."

"The herd? Oh very good Charles, yes, we are all a part of it are we not?"

"Not… all of us dear Annette. Now, can I get you a cup of hot beans?"

Annette laughed, "Hot beans? You are so funny Charles and sometimes I think you do not realise that you are."

"I am glad that you think that I am humorous, I was the life and soul of the party so to speak once."

"You are definitely that, how about we skip the hot beans and head out to your manor eh?"

"Whatever you want my sweet, your meal should be ready now."

Vaag left money for his drink on the table and then the two of them went to his car in the basement car-park.

***

Within twenty minutes or so, Vaag and Annette were seated in the small dining room, one at each end of the table.

"Your Moonlux Manor is simply outstanding and so divine Charles but do we have to sit so far apart?"

"This is not the main banquet hall Annette but I still like to follow etiquette."

"Of course my good sir" Annette replied with humour as she waved her hand. She was wearing an attractive tight fitting white dress that had splits up both of the lower sides. Vaag was wearing a dark navy suit with a white shirt and blue tie. The background music he had chosen was Mozart which they listened to as they drank Champagne from a large chilled ice bucket.

At eight pm precisely, as arranged, Jenna came into the dining room pushing a small trolley. Jenna was dressed in black dress and had used Ella's make-up that she had found in the bottom of the clothes bag that Vaag had given her, she now easily looked like she was in her early twenties.

"Oh and who is this beautiful young lady Charles? I was expecting an old and half bald doddery butler but I should have known better."

"This is my maid and our chef for tonight."

"Well isn't she the talented one" said Annette and she then held out her hand to Jenna who had just placed a small bowl of hot soup in front of her, "I'm Annette Stephens from Boston and who are you my lovely?"

Annette shook Jenna's hand and she noticed that Jenna was trembling slightly.

"Jenna… Shaw ma'am" Jenna said then she looked at Vaag in horror, she suddenly sensed that she should have not said her name but Vaag just looked stone-faced at her.

Annette looked puzzled for a moment, "I… seem to recognise that name from somewhere?"

Jenna was instantly alarmed, *He'll kill me, kill us both now for sure!* but then Jenna thought of something… "You must be thinking of Glenna Shaw ma'am, the famous romance author? A lot of people get our names mixed up."

"Oh… yes, of course, how silly of me."

Annette Stephens was lying, she had never heard of that author but she did not want to seem ignorant, especially to a maid.

A sudden thought hit Jenna though, *If the lady checks out the author then she will realise that the author does not exist and that might prompt her to search my name.*

"Jamaican fish soup ma'am, my grandmother's recipe and you really must check out that best-selling author's new book."

"That's real quaint and tasty too I bet and yes, I think I will buy that author new book, thank you" Annette said as she dipped her spoon into the hot bowl.

Jenna then quickly put the main course onto the hot plates at the side of the table.

"Jamaican steak for your main course, I will be back later with dessert" Jenna said then she scurried out of the dining room as fast as she could.

"Poor thing, she seems so nervous."

"It is… the first time she has cooked for anyone other than me."

"Oh I see… she is very pretty, is she to be our dessert then Charles?" Annette asked and suddenly there was a sexual undertone to her voice, "I do enjoy a black maid now and then."

Vaag became instantly aroused by Stephen's words, he imagined the three of them on Richarde's king size bed, he heard their erotic moans as the black and white women pleasured each other; then he was having sex with the both of them, pushing hard inside one then the other until they both came at the same time…

"That would be so much fun, maybe that can be arranged but I never force Jenna to do anything."

Vaag was lying through his sharp teeth and he was enjoying it, he would eat Jenna's food but his real main meal was not the Jamaican steak.

After the delicious main course, Jenna returned with a Jamaican Rum ice cream. After she had placed the dessert bowl in front of Vaag she left a small folded note with it. She had really been tempted to somehow do the same with Stephens, to leave a 'help me' note but she knew that if Vaag found out about it she would be dead as Stephens would soon be.

Stephens had not noticed the note and when Vaag discreetly opened it after Jenna had left the room, it simply read, 'Please do not kill her master Vaag, she is nice.'

Vaag folded the note and put it into his top pocket…
Suddenly he raised his hand slightly
Compounding the air around Stephens
So tight that she could not move
Vaag stood up from the table
And went to her
Only her eyes could move
Looking at him in complete horror
Her mouth trembling but no words could come out
Vaag bit into her wrist first
And drank the warm blood
Then he slit her throat with a sharp dinner knife
And immersed his head in the fountain of blood
Almost as if he was showering in it
Drinking in it
A complete bloodlust
As he looked into the frozen eyes of Stephens
And her horrified soul…

…

"What is it Charles, you seem to be daydreaming?"

"Yes… I think I was."

Vaag's hand was now flat on the table.

"Must be this delicious ice cream; for a moment there I thought I froze, like I could not move?"

"Yes, it must have been the dessert."

"So what's next, supper?" Annette asked and there was a sexy glint in her eyes.

"I… know the kind of supper you like" replied Vaag and suddenly he heard Charles Richarde's voice in his mind…

Do not do it!

Vaag had never experienced anything like this before, it was as if Richarde was still alive within him somehow.

And that was a worry for Vaag, he could not let Richarde regain control of his body at any cost.

But this was something that Vaag would contemplate and worry about later.

He decided that he would have sex with Stephens again and then he would decide if she would be supper or not.

VINCENT

After acquiring a large amount of blood from the field of cows, Ella returned to Starry Night. She calculated that she had enough blood for three days which she stored in one of Vincent's fridges that was used mainly for alcoholic drinks. Ella then went back to Vincent's bedroom and joined him in bed. Vincent was still suffering from an intense fever, one minute he was ice cold and the next his body was burning up. This worried Ella, she remembered similar symptoms that she had experienced when she had transformed into a Luxar but they did not seem as extreme as what Vincent was suffering.

Ella continued to wipe Vincent's brow with a cold wet cloth when he was feverish and then she would hold him tight to keep him warm when the ice shivers came. It was not until midday when Vincent opened his eyes. Ella had prepared a cold bottle of blood for him and held it to his lips as he wearily lifted his head from the pillow…

"Drink my love, the blood will ease the fever."

"Was… it like this… for you?" Vincent asked weakly after the refreshing blood had flowed down his throat.

"The blood of Lu'na is stronger than Charles' blood. You will need to be stronger than I was to get through this Vincent."

"I... will try..."

"Do not think about the threat of Charles, your health and well-being through this transformation is more important."

"I... do not want to let you down."

"You will not let me down Vincent, do not even think that. Here, drink more blood and then sleep until the fever has passed."

Vincent drank all of the blood in the bottle then lay his head back down on the pillow, he felt helpless, he felt scared, a fire like no other was raging inside of him. Once again he fell unconscious and once again red tears came to Ella's eyes.

***

Wednesday morning and Vincent woke up early. Ella was still sleeping next to him, she was nearly as exhausted as Vincent was but she had refilled the bottle of blood. Vincent felt slightly better and sat up quietly so as not to wake Ella. He drank the blood and felt instantly stronger although his body was still burning, as if there were a flame inside of him that needed to be released.

Vincent went for a long cold shower and when he returned to the bedroom, Ella was dressed and waiting for him.

"Do you feel stronger now my love?" Ella asked Vincent.

As Vincent slowly dressed in a white t-shirt and jeans he replied, "Yes... I do but it feels like there is something inside of me that is bursting to get out."

"The Fire... it is trying to control you, consume you, you must learn to control it. Come with me to the rear garden."

Ella and Vincent went to the back of Starry Night and to the right of Vincent's art studio, there was nothing in front of them but open farm fields and trees and importantly there was nobody about. As the sun came out from behind the clouds Ella and Vincent's skin turned white and hard...

"My hands" Vincent muttered, "they're like marble."

"As hard as marble too Vincent. Now, I want you to concentrate, feel the heat build up inside of you."

Vincent began to try and focus, he imagined the flames inside of him growing bigger, like he was a giant furnace...

"Like a demon" he said.

"Yes, let the demon out, let the flames fly free!"

Suddenly, Vincent's skin was like a living fire, white flames moved across his body like he was on fire. With all the mental strength he could muster, Vincent tried to set free the flaming fire from within him...

But it did not come

There was nothing at first
Nothing but that burning body heat
That was rising
Hotter and hotter
As the heat circulated his body
Like a whirlwind
That was slowly increasing
As it swirled
Round and round
Inside of him
Until Vincent thought that he would burst open
Explode like a living bomb
On the spot
And when he could not stand the heat any longer
He cried out
His voice as loud as a giant in pain
And white flames shot from his outstretched hands
Like a deadly fiery missile
A wave of white flame
That burnt a deep path through the wheat fields in front of him
It was as if the earth had suddenly opened
And was about to swallow everything
Taking it all to a flaming Hell…
Vincent fell backwards
His marble body sweating red droplets
Ella reached down to Vincent immediately
Worried that it had been too much for him…
"I… did it" Vincent mumbled as he fought to retain consciousness.
But… at what cost my love thought Ella.
Ella lifted Vincent up and hurried with him back to the house and up to the bedroom. Vincent was now unconscious and Ella was worried that he might die.

BULMER

The earliest flight Bulmer could get back to the United Kingdom was at 21.30pm, arriving at 02.15am Thursday morning. He had not phoned Davis about what he had found, he decided that he wanted to speak to him face to face after showing him the remains of Rolf.

There was nothing to do then but to eat and drink and think while he waited for his flight and he knew that he had quite a bit of thinking to do.

***

By 03.00am the next morning, Bulmer was home and in bed. At 07.30am he was awake and phoning Bob Davis to tell him that he had returned from Tenerife.

"Hey Bull, you're back, I thought that I would have heard from you while you there?"

"I… decided that it had to wait until I got back."

"What did?"

"Look Bob, can you come here before you go to work, it's very important pal?"

"Sure Bull, I was just about to leave, I'll be there soon."

When Davis arrived at Bulmer's house, Bumer took him to the dining room where he had laid out Rolf's face and hand skins on the table.

"Fucking Hell Bull… is that?"

"Rolf… or what's left of him."

Davis was astounded and struggled to immediately grasp what Rolf's remains might mean.

"But… if that is what is left of Rolf then…"

"Then I think the killer returned to the yacht."

"And… killed Cathy Rolf and Laing? But…"

"I think the killer is not human Bob, there was no burnt body on the altar. I think that altar thing killed Rolf and took his shape, drank his insides and took his memories."

"You're fucking kidding me Bull? Surely no such thing exists!"

"Think about it logically Bob; step by step, then it begins to make sense."

"But what do you think Cooky will make of it, he will think that you have gone fucking mad like the rest of the department!"

"That is why I am not telling him yet, not until we have investigated this."

"Wait, you mean…"

"That's right, the trail leads to Eastley and remember how fucking weird she seemed, the strange things that she said?"

"Dear Lord, you're telling me that Eastley is some sort of shape-shifting fucking vampire?"

"I don't know Bob, something like that. I know it's fucking unbelievable but I think we need to go and see her again… and now."

Davis was still struggling to come to terms with what Bulmer was saying, what he had told him but it all did make some kind of weird warped sense…

"I'm wearing a crucifix Bull, how about you?" Davis joked to try and relieve the nervous tension he felt inside, he felt that there was noway he could take this too serious yet though because it was just too unbelievable.

"My usual Saint Christopher… you get the wooden stake and hammer."

Bulmer looked stone faced at Davis but the humour in his eyes gave it away.

"Fucking Hell man" was all Davis could say then, "Okay Van Helsing, are you driving?"

EASTLEY RESIDENCE

Driving to Janet Eastley's house in Whitburn, Davis remembered something that he had wanted to tell Bulmer.

"There is something I wanted to mention to you Bull, it probably did not make the news in Tenerife."

Bulmer concentrated on his driving but he was intrigued by what Davis was about to tell him.

"What's that then Bob, another murder?"

"Not, exactly… something a young girl released on social media about her friend getting abducted, part of a video chat."

"And what has that to do with our cases Bob?"

"I don't know Bull, it's just bloody weird that's all… there's this guy at the moment of the attack and he's all white, like he's made of fucking marble or something and they're calling him the 'White Statue' now; it's huge on the internet, thousands of hits… the Durham police are looking into it."

"White Statue?"

"Aye, like a living statue, they reckon he was naked too."

"That's all we need, another fucking horror story!"

"I… was just wondering, if somehow it was connected to…"

"Whatever we are chasing?"

"Yeah."

"I just don't know Bob, maybe Eastley will be able to answer that. You got your gun with you?"

"No, it's back at the office" replied Davis realising that he must have sounded like some amateur private 'dick' detective.

"It's okay man I have mine."

"But does it have silver bullets Bull?" Davis joked.

"That's the stuff Bob, keep cracking them, we're gonna need a sense of humour I think."

As they approached Eastley's house they noticed that the front gates were open.

"Strange" said Bull immediately, "Wonder why they are not closed?"

"I thought they were automatic?"

"I think the car has to pass through them to close, she must have opened them then changed her mind?"

At the top of the drive they noticed that Eastley's car was parked at the front door. Bulmer rang the doorbell but there was no answer, he tried to open the door but it was locked.

"Let's go round the back" said Bulmer as he withdrew his gun from his shoulder holster.

Again the back garden was deserted and there was no sign of Eastley but this time the back door was open. Once inside, Bulmer and Davis checked all the rooms and eventually Bulmer noticed something in the kitchen, it was Eastley's diary, "Okay, we'll take this. She's obviously not here, although it's strange her car is, let's check it."

The car was not locked either and this immediately alerted Bulmer, "Check the boot there will ya Bob."

Davis opened it, then stepped back in horror…

"What is it Bob?"

Davis had froze on the spot like he was a statue.

"An… other fucking skin man, that's what!"

It was the remains of Charles Richarde.

"Fucking Hell Bob" said Bulmer as he looked down at the gruesome face of Richarde was was staring blankly up at him, the eye sockets black and empty as if his soul had been sucked right out of them.

"Get a bin bag from the kitchen Bob, I'll check inside the car for anything else."

After photographing and placing Richarde's body skin into the black bag Bulmer asked, "Any idea who this guy is?"

"Nope… but that would mean…"

"That whoever he is, Eastley is now him."

"Jesus Christ Bull, this is just fucking crazy man!"

Davis was shaking his head in total disbelief, as if he now found himself in some dark daytime nightmare in which they were chasing a real monster.

"I know… but we gotta keep our cool man. Look, you go back to HQ, don't tell them that I am back or about what we have found and know now. I'll send you the picture of this poor guy's grisly face, see if you can somehow find out who he is before we have to go down the official fingerprint route. I'll look through this diary, there might be a clue in there somewhere."

JENNA

"Hello Jenna, are you there?"

Jenna was sitting in front of the television, watching, hoping that somehow there would be news that the police now knew where she was but of course there was none.

Vaag's voice on her small Walkie-Talkie made her jump.

Then her skin began to crawl…

"Yes, master… I am here."

Where else would I be you twisted evil bastard!

"Good, good. Your door is unlocked I thought that we could talk again in the conservatory?"

Jenna instantly began to shake.

"But do not worry, no nasty needles and no sleepy serums, just you and me and a bottle of wine maybe?"

"I'll… be right there master."

Jenna could not stop shaking, she went to the toilet to be sick but nothing came from her stomach.

He killed her… he's going to kill me now! I must do as he says, I must be a good servant, a good servant, a good servant…

Jenna bathed her face in cold water. She was wearing jeans and a t-shirt but she changed into the black dress she had been wearing the night before. She then hastily applied eye shadow and lipstick, Jenna wanted to look good for Vaag.

Before going to the conservatory, Jenna went to the kitchen for a bottle of wine and two glasses, he had mentioned the wine so she thought that it might please him.

At the conservatory, Vaag had closed all the sun blinds, he was aware that his white skin and red eyes might unsettle Jenna and he was not in the mood for doing that, in fact he was feeling aroused in a sexual way but that was not the main reason for wanting to speak to his servant. As Jenna approached in her black dress, Vaag's arousal increased.

"Ah Jenna, how beautiful you look, that dress is the perfect fit and you do have the most wonderful bodily figure."

Vaag eyed Jenna from top to bottom and this sickened Jenna but she had to force a smile.

"I… am glad that I please you, I have brought the wine you suggested my lord."

"I… think you will please me" said Vaag and his voice was low and sensual and disturbing to Jenna. These were indeed ominous words but Jenna knew that she had to do everything the monster wanted if she was survive.

"Sit beside me Jenna, on this sofa or is it a settee, I never know, this language has many words for one thing. Put the wine and glasses on the table in front of us and relax, I have more or less decided something."

Jenna did as she was told and it was Vaag who poured out the wine. He was silent for a moment then he sipped his wine.

"I want to make a toast to you Jenna for your superb meal last night. I don't think that I have heard of this Jamaica though, maybe I have been there in another age but it could have been called something else."

"My… grandmother came from there" said Jenna meekly, aware that she had not relaxed and was shaking slightly.

"Yes, you said that last night."

"And… the lady, did she…"

"She left this morning with a wide smile on her face. She is fine, I resisted the urge to… well, not all my urges."

Vaag began to laugh and Jenna tried to smile as if she understood the sick joke that Vaag was making.

"Maybe you will cook for us again soon?"

"I… would like that" Jenna lied but she was happy that the woman had survived.

"Good, so here is to you Jenna on a job well done."

Vaag raised his glass and Jenna did so too, she was still trembling though as she drank her wine.

"Not better than blood but it will do for now" Vaag had to add and Jenna almost had to force Vaag's words from her mind..

Vaag was wearing an open white shirt and black trousers and as he put his glass down on the table he moved closer to Jenna, she wanted to get up and run but she knew that it would be pointless, she knew that it would enrage Vaag and that could be fateful.

Strangely, the scent of Vaag did not repulse Jenna like she expected it to, he had obviously used Richarde's aftershave which had an almost comforting effect on her. Vaag then placed his his hand on her bare knee and began to rub it gently.

"Do you enjoy being my servant now?" Vaag asked and the tone of his voice softened.

"Yes… master I do."

Lie, lie to him…

"So you like to serve me?"

Jenna nodded but her eyes were looking down, looking bleakly into her wine glass.

"Maybe I can do something for you, something to please you?"

Jenna's eyes opened wider.

No, no, no…

Vaag's hand moved gently up Jenna's short skirt and began to slowly caress her there. She wanted to cross her legs but she did not, she remained brave and looked Vaag in the face. Richarde was obviously much older than Jenna but for the first time she realised that he was in fact quite a handsome man.

"Does that please you Jenna?" Vaag said increasing the intensity of his touch.

"Yes… master" and Jenna's voice gasped as she said this, Vaag's stimulation with his hand was beginning to have an effect on her even though she was fighting the sensual feeling with all her heart.

"Good, and that pleases me, life is for living and you should feel pleasure as often as you can."

Vaag's hand had now entered Jenna and Vaag was excited by how wet she was. He pushed himself up against her and kissed her gently not noticing that her eyes were wet too. Jenna was surprised by how fresh and clean Vaag's breath smelt, it was how she imagined it to be, the breath of a dragon, the breath of a monster which was now panting heavily in her ear.

"I want to hear your pleasure, feel your delight as you tighten around my hand."

Vaag was moving his hand in and out now with urgency, causing Jenna to climax in an erotic frenzy that was unexpected and degrading for Jenna.

"There.. there my dear, I know how much you enjoyed that and now I want you to please me."

Vaag unzipped his trousers and pushed Jenna's head towards his penis that was now exposed to her…

"No… no, please master."

"Surely you mean yes?" replied Vaag and he pushed her head further down on him and Jenna opened her mouth and took him into her.

Vaag moved inside of Jenna's mouth but he knew that he was too big for her, "That is good servant, you serve me well, I shall reward you now with my seed."

Vaag withdrew from Jenna's mouth and entered her between the legs…

And began to pump at her hard.

"You are so young, so sweet… maybe you can be my queen one day" Vaag whispered as his thrusting intensity increased. All of Jenna's body began to shake, she had not had sexual intercourse before and she felt totally ashamed that she was actually enjoying it…

She began to drift away

To another world

To Vaag's world

A world full of naked men and women

Moving together in an endless orgy

Savage and sensual

These were Vaag's thoughts

That had entered the mind of Jenna

Seducing her and tempting her to join in

To cast away her innocence

And to divulge in the pleasures of the flesh

To do things she had never known

Never imagined

And she gave herself to her desires

To his desire

With wild abandon

Like a lost soul

Lost in her erotic passion

Never to return…

And this time when she came

It was as if she was floating

Above a white marble statue

Whose large erect penis was now hard within her

And as Vaag ejaculated into her

Her body seemed to explode
Then implode with an immense pleasure
She had never know before
Every nerve ending tingling with passion and desire
Like she was a live wire
Like an unknown living electricity
Was flowing through her
And she wanted more
She did not want Vaag to stop
But this is wrong
This is a lie
This is not love
But this is survival...
And Vaag started to push within her again saying,
"You are the little slut I needed"
But there was no malice in his voice, he was just trying to be erotic and Jenna was surprised that she was pleased by this. Jenna was now someone else, an older Jenna, a Jenna of the future perhaps, a more experienced Jenna maybe...
But this is not love
This is survival
She kept thinking
And these thoughts comforted her during her ordeal

And after a long time they came together once again.
And Vaag seemed almost satisfied, he contemplated entering Jenna from behind in her anus but then he thought that he would keep that *little delight* for the next time. Jenna's sexual education was something he was now looking forward to enjoying to the very utmost, he was now determined to show his young slave a new world of ecstasy and desire a world she would never want to leave.
Vaag rolled off the exhausted Jenna and zipped up his trousers while she adjusted her dress...
At least I am not dead, I am still here, still alive she thought with relief but she she did feel ashamed, disgusted with herself because *have I enjoyed what Vaag has just done to me?*
Jenna felt sick again, wanted to run again from the nightmare she was in then she remembered something, something that Vaag had said when she had first entered the conservatory. Jenna thought that now Vaag had had his way with with her, he might discard her, might get bored with her and kill her; she knew that she had to keep interacting with him.
Jenna finished her glass of wine to steady her nerves.
"Master, you said that you had decided something?"

"Oh yes, that is right, there was something else other than our carnal desires."

And once again Vaag laughed and Jenna tried her best to join in.

"It was something that I thought you would like but I have not got it for you yet, I need to find the right one."

"Like a surprise?"

"Yes my dear girl, just like a surprise."

Once again, Jenna did not like the sound of this and once again she lied.

"That will be nice master."

"Yes, it will I think. Now, I could stay here and fuck you all day, would you like that?"

Jenna was disgusted again but she knew that he actually meant it, "Yes… of course master, whatever you desire of me I will do."

"That is music to my ears, I think the saying is" laughed Vaag but then he became serious, "I could fuck you all day and all night but I need to feed I think, we do not want my hunger to turn on you, do we my sweet pea?"

Jenna shivered.

"No… master."

"That is what I wanted to hear because I do think that we may have much more sex together, I know that there is more for you to learn about pleasing me in bed and maybe there are new things that I will learn from you hopefully? It will be so much fun finding out those things my dear and I am now really looking forward to it as you should be also. But now you must return to your cosy habitat and I must go to satisfy my other desires and maybe find your secret surprise too."

ALICE

Like Ella, Alice was worried about Vincent. She knew that Ella had never left his side and that they had been in the garden for Vincent to try and come to terms with the Luxar Fire but she had respected their privacy at this time and simply hoped for the best.

Something else was worrying Alice though, she had heard a report on the news about the sighting of a living 'White Statue' and the disappearance of the young girl Jenna Shaw. Alice had wanted to tell Ella about it but she knew that it was best to wait for the right time.

At midday, Ella did leave the bedroom and Vincent and went down to the kitchen, she was exhausted, more mentally than physically and what she needed was some of the blood that was in Vincent's beer fridge. Alice was sitting at the kitchen table when Ella entered the room.

"Hi Ella, how is he and how are you?"

"I'm fine, at least I will be after a pint of blood. I am worried about Vincent though, he is still feverish, it was as if letting out the Fire was too much for him yesterday. What I fear now is that Lu'na's blood and power is too strong for Vincent."

"Do you really think that it is?"

"I hope not, I think the next few hours will be crucial and I need to be at his side. But enough of our troubles, how are you Alice, and Rocky?"

"Oh, Rocky is fine, Killer the cat keeps him occupied I think judging by the noises I hear and I… feel safe here I guess."

"That is good, but I sense something else in your voice."

"It's… I don't know if it is the right time to tell you?"

"Please go on Alice, do not keep anything from me."

"Okay, I was going to keep it until Vincent was better."

"What is it Alice?"

"I don't know if you have seen any news reports recently?"

"I have not watched any television, I have only cared for Vincent."

"Of course you have…" Alice paused for a moment then continued, "You will not have seen the report about the White Statue then?"

"White Statue?"

Alice told Ella about the abduction and disappearance of the teenager Jenna Shaw and her friend's strange video which was now getting a lot of exposure on social media worldwide. Ella immediately Googled it all on her phone…

"Dear God!" exclaimed Ella, "That has to be Charles… and they have not found her body yet, I… think he may have abducted her, taken her to Moonlux Manor?"

"Why do you think that?"

"Because I think she is the 'surprise' Charles has for me. I keep saying Charles but but I am certain now that he is the creature called Vaag. I must never say Charles again, it disrespects his name."

Ella felt a sudden sadness hit her heart.

"So you think she is alive then?"

"I think that there is a good chance that she is because if Vaag had the bloodlust that poor girl would have been found dead on that lonely track, with all of her blood sucked from her."

"That is absolutely gruesome!" replied Alice but she was pleased that she was hearing a new determination in Ella's voice, "I sense something in your voice now Ella, surely you are not contemplating going to Moonlux Manor?"

"I feel I must now because that young girl's life is definitely in danger."

"But by yourself? You told me that you would need the 'Fire' to defeat this so-called Vaag creature?"

"It is a chance I must take, maybe I can fool Vaag, maybe tell him that you have recovered and that I have returned to Moonlux then maybe I can set the girl free somehow? Will you monitor and look after Vincent for me Alice?"

"Of course I will… but what if he wakes up and asks where you are?"

"Tell him… anything but do not tell him that I have gone to Moonlux."

ELLA

Ella took her BMW and raced as fast as she dared to Moonlux Manor and as she approached the imposing residence her heart began to race too. She parked at the front doors and entered the house in in an almost frantic pace completely forgetting to lock the doors behind her. Her adrenalin was pumping because of the threat of Vaag but her Luxar senses indicated that he was not in the manor. She then listened for any other movement, any other indication of life and she heard the faint sound of a human heart beating in the tower basement…

The girl Jenna… yes, that is where he would keep her.

The basement key was where Richarde usually kept it, on the table in his recreational room. Ella opened the door and descended the curved stairway and was surprised by the girl in the basement who seemed to be waiting for her.

"Who… are you, where is Vaag?"

Before leaving Starry Night, Ella had showered and changed into jeans and a red t-shirt which had the words LOVE IS ALL THAT MATTERS printed on it in sparkling white.

"You know his real name then?" asked Ella who was surprised by Jenna's words.

"Of course, he told me everything but who are you, are you his queen?"

"I am no queen Jenna, I am a friend of Charles Richarde, the real Richarde."

Jenna stepped back, suddenly she seemed afraid, "Are… you one of those white monsters then?"

"I am not a monster… but yes, I am what Richarde was but not what Vaag is. I am here to take you home."

"But… what about Vaag?" Jenna stuttered, shaking now because she could not believe that she was about to be truly set free."

"Vaag is not here, I do not know where he is but it seems we have a window now for your escape."

"We are going to escape out of the window?" replied Jenna and Ella had to smile at her naive comment.

"No, we are going out of the front door to my BMW."

"Fuck, I'm leaving this shit-hole in style then!"

And this time Ella had to laugh.

"It is good that you have kept up your spirit Jenna… did Vaag harm you at all?"

"No… he… just touched me."

Ella instantly knew what Jenna was implying.

"The bastard! But at least you are still alive my dear, now we must hurry!"

Ella grabbed Jenna's hand and they quickly ascended the stairs… only to be greeted by two men at the top, both with guns in their hands which were pointed at Ella.

"Okay lady, release the girl or I will shoot" said the eldest man and he looked and sounded like he meant business.

Ella released Jenna's hand then asked "Who are you?" as the obvious penny had not dropped.

"We are policemen Bulmer and Davis and who the fuck are you?"

"I'm Ella Newman, a friend of Charles Richarde. I am here to save Jenna."

"You're not one of those fucking cannibal creatures are you?" asked Davis and he sounded real nervous.

"No, I am Charles Richarde's assistant but Charles is unfortunately not what he was. How did you know that the creature is now Charles?"

"Police work lady" said Bulmer proudly, "I found Rolf's skin in the Canary Islands and I checked one of the victim's diary, Richarde's name was in there and we found his skin. Routine work basically."

"Then you have done well officer."

"Detective... and I think we should take Jenna now."

"Of course, because..."

Ella suddenly stopped talking and she looked to the recreational room door. Bulmer and Davis lowered their guns and looked at the same door then Bulmer asked, "Because what?"

"Because Vaag might return at any moment."

And Ella's voice now sounded ominous, fearful even.

"Vaag, is that the creature's name?" Bulmer had to ask.

"Yes, and now... he is here."

"What!" exclaimed Davis and both detectives raised their guns again.

"Shit Bull, what do we do now?" asked Davis who was now beginning to almost panic.

"You take the girl, I'll get this Vaag."

"Your bullets will have no effect, he will harden his skin" advised Ella.

"Not if I shoot him first."

"But he has the speed of a Luxar."

"Don't know what a Luxar is but at least I will distract him while Bob gets away with the girl. Where is the bastard?"

"He is in the banquet hall, come with me and I will show where it is, you will need my help to try and defeat him."

"Okay Jenna sweetheart, come with me, you are going home now" Davis said, eager to get away from Moonlux Manor as fast as he could.

Suddenly Jenna froze, refusing to go with Davis, "No... no, Vaag will kill you all, you do not know hat he is, he is my master and he is a monster!"

Ella realised immediately that to some degree, Jenna had been brainwashed by Vaag but it was Bulmer who spoke next, "We know that girl, just do as my partner Davis tells you okay?" barked Bulmer who was rapidly losing his patience. The killer was there and he had to confront him.

"No wait... I think that I can... talk to him, maybe persuade him to go with you without any violence?" said Jenna hesitantly.

"And why do you think that Jenna?" Ella asked gently.

"Because... I think he loves me" was Jenna's blunt and surprising reply.

"That evil bastard could not love anybody" replied Bulmer with venom, "We are all just food fodder for him I think."

Ella held Jenna's shoulder but suddenly she bolted for the door.

"Where the fuck is she going?" shouted Bulmer.

"To her master, to try and save us, quick, follow me..." and Ella raced to the door to go to the banquet hall.

"Fuck Bull, what do we do now, what can we do?" asked Davis almost hinting that it would be better to leave the house of horrors that they were now in.

"We do what the lady said… and don't hesitate to shoot the fucking bastard!"

When they entered the banquet hall, Jenna was in Vaag's arms and in front of them on one of the tables was a young black man who was not moving. Bulmer and Davis immediately aimed both their guns at Vaag.

"Ah, the Detective Inspectors; I am impressed by your… police work."

Vaag's skin suddenly turned white and Bulmer and Davis simply gasped, their mouths wide open like two fishes about to bite the same hook.

"Let the girl go you bastard!" shouted Bulmer suddenly.

"Why should I, she does want to leave me, do you my love?" replied Vaag calmly, looking down at Jenna who was still cradled in his arms.

"No… no, I just don't want anybody to to die, that is all" she pleaded.

Vaag suddenly turned his red eyes toward Ella, "Ah, my lady Ella, I see that you have finally returned and what a beautiful specimen you are too."

"I am here for Jenna, Vaag… and to kill you."

"You speak honestly dear Ella, I would have expected nothing less from you but surely you do not think that you are more powerful than the might of Richarde and Vaag combined?"

"Maybe not…. but we shall see."

"We shall see indeed."

Suddenly, Bulmer shouted at Jenna, "Step away girl, step away now!"

Vaag gently pushed Jenna away from him, "Fire away Inspector Bulmer, let us see what effect your toy guns have."

Bulmer and Davis fired their guns at Vaag together but the bullets bounced off Vaag's marble hard body then dangerously around the hall.

"Stop shooting Bob!" shouted Bulmer immediately.

"Yes, stop dear Bob" Vaag said sarcastically and suddenly there was a heavy atmosphere in the hall, like an invisible presence had entered the large room. Vaag waved both of his hands and the two detectives were lifted off the ground and sent into the air against the painted glass windows, the reinforced glass did not break. The oppressive air around them kept them pinned tightly against the windows like helpless puppets, both men could just about talk and move their heads.

"Fuck… Bull, what… just happened?" stuttered a delirious Davis in disbelief then, "I… think I'm dying Bull."

"Fight… Bob, fight it."

Bulmer struggled bravely to move but he could not, it was as if Vaag had somehow super-glued him to the window.

Ella turned white and hard in reaction to what Vaag had done to the two policemen and then she sprang through the air at Vaag at great speed but Vaag was just as fast and with a great gush of air that had the power of a turbine wind tunnel he pushed Ella back against the wall next to the hall door.

"See how pathetic your so-called saviours are dear Jenna?" Vaag said triumphantly.

"Please… do not kill them master" stuttered Jenna who now had tears in her eyes and was now struggling to believe what she was actually seeing.

A sickly smile widened on Vaag's face, "No… I will not kill them now, I will keep them for when I am hungry, this is a banquet hall after all" and Vaag's mad manic laughter reverberated loudly around the large dining area.

Vaag then looked down at the black man on the table beside him.

"This is your 'surprise' Jenna, the gift I promised you and I did want to present him to you under better circumstances."

"Is… he dead" asked Jenna who was feeling quite sick now, her stomach tight with fear.

"No, just one of Doctor Richarde's sedatives. I will take him to your rooms in a mo…"

Vaag stopped talking suddenly, he had sensed another presence and in the hall doorway there was the shadow of a man. Ella managed to turn her head to where Vaag was looking.

"Vincent!" she shouted in surprise and dread, "You should not have come here!"

Vincent Harper stepped into the light of the hall…

"Wild horses would not have stopped me. When I woke up, Alice would not say where you were but I guessed… and I guessed right."

Vincent was wearing a light blue shirt but it was covered totally in sweat and he was obviously in a weak state, swaying on his feet like he was drunk.

"You should not be here Vincent, the fever still consumes you" pleaded Ella who was still battling to move the rest of her body but Vaag's control of the air around her was too strong.

"Well now, what have we here, two lovers perhaps? Let me check Richarde's mind for a moment… ah yes, I should have known, the human called Vincent Harper, so that is where you have been 'hiding' my naughty Ella?"

"I… am human no more, you evil creature, I am Luxar with the power of Lu'na within me" replied Vincent but his voice was broken and painful.

"Evil creature, am I an evil creature Jenna?" replied Vaag who then looked at Jenna who was still standing near to him although she was shaking more and more now from the shock of the events being played out in front of her.

Jenna reluctantly shook her head, it was obvious that she was now in a confused state of mind. Vaag turned his gaze back to Vincent.

"Yes Mister Harper I can see that you are no longer human, I see your white Luxar skin and it makes me wonder if the Luxar Elders know about this? I somehow think that they do not which does not bode well for you. And also you say that you have the Luxar power within you, but look at yourself, you can hardly stand on your feet?"

Vaag laughed again, he now seemed like a cat who was playing with the mouse it was about to kill.

Suddenly, Vincent's skin seemed to be covered in white flames, as if they were being reflected on him; it was obvious that the power of Lu'na had been ignited.

"No!" cried out Ella as she saw the Luxar Fire build up within him…

"I… have to try Ella" stuttered Vincent and he stretched out his shaking arms and released a bolt of white fire toward Vaag that crackled with an unearthly deadly silence, a fire that would have destroyed Vaag had it engulfed him.

But Vaag lifted his arms and hands with swiftness of Richarde's speed and sent a swirling ball of wind towards the flames, so strong that it pushed the deadly fire back into Vincent who staggered helplessly backwards to the left side of the door. He was burning internally now from the fire within him.

"No, please!" cried Ella again as Vaag sent another powerful rush of air to pin Vincent to the wall like Ella. The white couple with their arms spread wide looked like two macabre crucified statues

Vaag looked supremely satisfied with himself as he spoke to all of his captives, his voice booming from him like some mad dictator.

"The power of Vaag is great, I will make you all regret coming here tonight and you will be the first" he said looking towards Davis whose face was frozen with fear, "You will provide the blood I need this night" but again Jenna pleaded with her master for mercy…

"Please lord, please master, please let them go" and she wrapped her arms around Vaag's waist and hung on to him as if she were somehow about to drown.

"Do not plead for them Jenna, they are our enemies, a threat to our existence and will be treated as such."

Ella's head was down, again she struggled against the power of Vaag that was holding her but even she was not as strong as nature… then she heard something, something outside of the painted glass windows a strange crackling sound, a large flapping movement that was like the sound of giant bat wings…

LUCIFER

Vaag held Jenna's hand as he loosened her grip on him, he then began to make her caress the body of the still unconscious man on the table; making her rub his hair first, then his face, then his body and down to between his legs which was where Jenna pulled her hand away.

Vaag laughed but Jenna felt ashamed as she knew that Vaag's victims which seemed to her to be like doomed flies in a giant spider's web, were watching.

"He will be sedated for some time but I will take him down to your bedroom and you can fuck him when he wakes up I am sure that he will like that."

Ella's disgust of this vile creature Vaag boiled within her, "You treat humans worse than animals" she managed to say to Vaag.

Vaag turned toward Ella and his red eyes blazed with fury, "They are animals, animals that I feed on... that you want to feed on!"

"Never! I have never wanted to taste human blood."

"You lie Luxar witch, like Richarde, you both pose as some sort of human 'protectors' but I know your innermost desires."

"I am a Luxar now... but the blood that I want is yours, you fucking monster!" shouted Vincent with all the remaining strength he could muster.

Bulmer was still trying to come to terms with what he was seeing and hearing but he thought that young Vincent's comment were encouraging and extremely brave, "Good for you son, you tell that evil bastard!"

"Quiet human or it will be you that I eat first!"

"Do it then, kill me, then I'll come back and haunt you... and I'll fucking kill you somehow!"

Vaag just smiled with pity for the confused human.

"Hah, ghosts, spirits, there are no such things and if you did come back I would..."

Vaag stopped speaking suddenly, once again he was aware of a shadow in the hall doorway, a shadow that began to speak...

"You should believe in ghosts Vaag, they do come back to haunt you."

Vaag turned to the door, he could not see who it was but he vaguely recognised the voice. The man stepped into the light of the banquet hall and revealed himself to be Alan Rolf.

Bulmer and Davis gasped.

Vaag gasped.

"Rolf! But how can this be, I ate you, I drank your bones and then became you?"

"How can it be indeed?" Rolf replied as he slowly walked towards Vaag.

Davis managed to turn his head towards Bulmer, "Tell me that this is some sort of a nightmare Bull, please."

"I wish it was Bob... I can't believe what I am seeing here, maybe ghosts do exist, maybe he has come to save us?"

Rolf was quite near to Vaag now but Vaag was not stepping back, he was in a state of puzzled shock that was beginning to fill him with a strange intrigue.

"What does it feel like to be speaking to someone you killed, someone you ate, someone whose identity you stole?" asked Rolf coldly.

"What... are you?" was all that Vaag could muster.

"How about Cathy Rolf?"

And Rolf's body suddenly turned into his dead wife.

"Or maybe Salty Laing?"

And once again the same happened and it was Laing who was now looking at Vaag.

"What sort of witchcraft is this?" asked Vaag who, like all the others in the hall, was finding it hard to believe what he was witnessing.

Suddenly it was Janet Eastley that was standing in front of Vaag, looking him fiercely in the eye as she reached and caressed the side of

Vaag's stunned face, "You are a sexual predator Vaag; how about sex with me again, would you like that, how about fucking a cold dead woman and the maggots within me?"

And Vaag was now looking at the grey face of a rotting corpse with no eyes, the bone of the skull cutting through the nose and mouth...

Vaag turned away, he was feeling disgust at what the gruesome Eastley was saying and the horrific image of her, he could even smell her dead breath which was like green smoke from the fires of Hell.

Vaag steadied himself and then had to ask, "But... you are dead, you have to be, you certainly look and smell like it?"

"And me, am I dead or am I still alive inside of you?"

Vaag was now looking at Charles Richarde and Ella gasped...

"Charles... Charles, you live!"

Richarde turned to Ella and smiled as he tried to comfort her, "I will always live within you my child" then he turned back to Vaag who had started to laugh which was manic and confused and even fearful, it was the laugh of a totally bewildered mind.

"Are... you a magician, a wizard come to taunt me? Because if you are, your death is now near at hand."

"Shall we talk about death?"

And Richarde's voice had changed but Vaag did not recognise it immediately. It was a female voice, soft and alluring...

"I thought you were dead" Richarde continued and Vaag was now completely engrossed by what the man with the woman's voice was saying.

"I left too early, too heartbroken because I had not saved the love of my life... because I had burnt her lifeless skin with you."

Slowly Richarde's body dissolved and changed into a beautiful young woman in a golden gown and golden shoes, a woman with royal tiara on her head...

"My God!" Vaag gasped out loudly because this was a vision he had not expected.

"And what god do you pray to? You are a godless creature from beyond Hell."

The woman looked at Vaag like a spirit that had come to finally claim his soul.

"No... you are the one from Hell, you are the one known as Lucifer!" screamed Vaag and his voice echoed throughout the hall, "I... knew that you would come one day... but how did you find me?"

"Do you not know that you are world-wide news Vaag? Did you not know that you really should clean up after dinner?" the visage of the woman joked.

"The skins… on the boat" but how did you know about Richarde, I hid his skin in the boot of Eastley's car?"

"Since I arrived here, I have been following the police, I had supreme faith in them" the woman replied looking towards the totally stunned faces of Bulmer and Davis.

"Did I just hear that the Devil has been following us Bull?" said Davis, not believing what he had just heard.

"Fuck me… Bob" stuttered an exhausted Bulmer, "I'm fucking lost for words mate…"

"That's a first then my friend"

And both men managed a painful spluttering laugh.

Vaag however was not feeling remotely humorous, in fact there was the rare feeling of fear running through his veins.

"So you have come here to kill me then, revenge for what happened to you beloved Lanar… and she really was a delicious dish!"

Lucifer's hand reached out at lightning speed and grabbed Vaag's hard white neck.

"I am more powerful now Lucifer, I have the combined strength of a Luxar" Vaag stuttered through his gritted sharp teeth.

Vaag pushed Lucifer away from him with a gust of sharp wind and Lucifer was surprised by this new power.

"The power of air I see, the control of nature… but I have the power of Angelic Light."

"So that is how you managed your pathetic parlour tricks?"

"I am not here to entertain you Vaag… there are certain people who are interested in you; they want to know what you are, where you have come from. I dearly wanted to destroy you; to finally kill you, like you have killed so many, like you killed my Lanar… but I have reluctantly decided to do what they want."

Like a flash of lightning, Vaag lunged at Lucifer and grabbed him by the throat. Lucifer could feel the tightness of the air around him beginning to crush and bite at him but…

Lucifer turned into his real form

A blackened burnt body

With large wings of crackling black light

He did look like a dark demon from Hell

And everyone in the hall gasped again with what strength they had left…

"You have revealed your true self, I will enjoy crushing your demonic visage. I will be known not just as The Bone Drinker, I will be Vaag the Devil Killer!"

"Crush me?" shouted Lucifer and the walls of the hall seemed to shake with the might of his voice, "I am the Fallen Angel, I have angelic powers, no pathetic bone drinking shape-shifting cannibal creature will prevail against me!"

Lucifer waved his hand at Vaag and suddenly there was an orb of dazzling light around Vaag's head making Vaag stagger back in, totally surprised by what was happening to him...

"You cannot see, can you Vaag? You will now only see what I want you to see, images of all the humans you have ate, of all their corpses coming to eat you, like hungry zombies. It is what you deserve evil one."

Vaag was dazed and confused, he could no longer control the air around Lucifer and his other captives. Ella, Vincent, Bulmer and Davis all slumped slowly to the floor while Jenna began to cringe in terror in the corner of the hall, seeing and hearing the Devil was just too much for her young mind to absorb.

Then the body of Lucifer increased in size as he grabbed the disorientated body of Vaag who was sending out waves of air in a blind fury but his focus and concentration was no longer available to him, the air just rebounded around the hall like the lost wind in a field.

But then Vaag realised that they maybe a way out of Lucifer's spell and his hand suddenly pointed skyward to release a burst of white light from the large white ring on his finger...

"He's trying to open a portal with the Luxstone ring, he's trying to escape!" cried out Ella as she tightly hugged Vincent who was fighting to remain conscious.

The large ebony fingers of Lucifer tore the ring from Vaag and threw it to Ella on the floor, "Trinkets, he will have no need for such jewellery now."

Lucifer's enlarged arm wrapped tightly around Vaag's white neck, "I leave you now brave humans, Vaag is no longer a threat to you" and suddenly the black light on Lucifer's back that resembled great wings began to flap and he took flight through one of the large painted glass windows, taking out part of the wall as he flew up towards the moon.

ELLA

As Ella helped the weakened Vincent to his feet, Bulmer did the same with Davis.

"Fucking Hell Bull, I'm gonna change my job" said Davis in a humourless dulcet tone of voice.

"Not exciting enough for you Bob?"

And both men tried to laugh but they were still in pain from the power of Vaag's crushing wind.

"How are you my love?" asked Ella but she knew that Vincent was still fighting to remain conscious.

"I'm fine… I think I need a drink"

"You need blood then?"

"No… a bottle of Newcastle Brown Ale and a whiskey chaser please" he quipped and Ella managed a smile but she knew that Vincent needed immediate rest. Then she saw the quivering state of Jenna and went straight to her and helped her stand up. Ella then took Jenna to a seat but not at the table on which the black boy was still sleeping.

"What… what has just happened?" asked a confused shaking Jenna.

"I… think that you should try and not think about it."

Bulmer and Davis staggered together to where Jenna was seated.

"How are you pet?" asked Bulmer of Jenna.

"She is in shock" Ella had to say.

"She is not the only one... I mean, the fucking Devil for Christsakes, did that really just happen?"

Bulmer then looked at the large gaping hole in the wall and realised that it had indeed happened.

Ella grabbed Bulmer's arm and took him to one side, "Are you going to report what has happened this night Detective Bulmer?"

Bulmer thought for a moment...

"I.. don't know... I mean, who would fucking believe me anyway; and look at you, you're as white as marble!"

Ella turned her skin back to flesh.

"I am worried about Jenna, she cannot go home... in this state."

"The police can deal with trauma victims obviously but what do you suggest?" asked Bulmer and he was intrigued by what this being that he now knew to be something called a Luxar, was going to suggest.

"Can I have you and your friends word that you will not report this, it will affect my work here as a Protector."

"Protector?"

"I will tell you all you want to know if you do as I ask."

Bulmer thought for a moment then replied, "Okay vampire lady, you have our word but what about Jenna, about what she has experienced here?"

"I think she needs to go to a place called The New Sanctuary, there will be specialist help there for her, help that she could get nowhere else and they have advanced hypnotheraphy there; I will guarantee you that she will have no recollection of Vaag or what happened here. Jenna will then be able to return and live a normal life again."

"But her abduction by the 'White Statue'?"

"Unexplained."

"Like an alien abduction you mean?"

Ella smiled, "Possibly, but I guarantee there will be no mental trauma for her."

"And the sleeping boy on the table?"

"He goes to the Sanctuary too, he will get the same treatment."

Bulmer smiled, "Okay then, it's a deal... and I only hope that I can deal with the nightmares."

"Oh, I think you will Detective Bulmer, you seem to be a strong character."

"I fucking know I am pet" and he smiled and winked at Ella, "Right, let's sort this all out, then I'm going to the pub with Bob to tell him that he has to keep his big mouth shut and you're going to this place called The New Sanctuary."

"Yes Detective…" but then Ella began to think of something that Bulmer had said earlier, "But wait though, didn't you tell me that you have Charles Richarde's skin?"

"That's right, it was in the boot of Janet Eastley's car."

Ella's face lit up and suddenly there was a wide smile on her face as she looked at the Luxstone ring in her hand…

"That is good, that is very good!"

Richard Valanga
The Alamo
Washington
9/7/2022
17.03pm
In the garden
In the sun.

My Young Adult novella The Sunderland Vampire was an exercise in fun, a break from my never ending Complex Hell which I was writing at the time. Initially there was no planning, no synopsis, it was an experiment in spontaneous imagination that did eventually develop into a paranormal mystery with a definite plot and storyline.

And the characters stayed in my mind until this sequel began to develop. And make no mistake, there is a much more adult approach to this novel that is more in line with my current writing for this sort of genre with an exciting variety of characters that now take me to a follow up story called Lust For Life where I explore the individuality of the main personalities and their origins.

I do wish to say that Bloodlust has probably been my most enjoyable novel to date, I have absolutely loved writing this novel and hopefully this shows in the result and I do feel that I have a truly unique evil character with the ancient and deadly Vaag The Bone Drinker.

Having now started Lust For Life, the enjoyment continues…

Richard Valanga
8/8/2022

ACKNOWLEDGEMENTS

Many thanks to all of you who have reviewed my books with positive and favourable comments, your feedback is a great inspiration to me. And grateful thanks to all that have shared my work on social media, cheers, it really means a lot to me!

1 - PXFuel, Jacket cover photograph.
2 - Google Translate.
3 - Basic Instinct.
4 - Route 66 Aftershave.
5 - Sabbath Bloody Sabbath, Black Sabbath.
6 - Doctor Strange, Marvel.
7 - Complex Heaven, Richard Valanga.
8 - Lux, Brian Eno.
9 - A Hard Rain's A-Gonna Fall, Bob Dylan, Bryan Ferry.
10 - Captain Marvel, Marvel Comics.
11 - Sympathy For The Devil, The Rolling Stones.
12 - Roxy Music's Bryan Ferry and Paul Thompson.

13 - Let's Rock, The Black Keys.
14 - Stop, Black Rebel Motorcycle Club.
15 - Peter Cushing, Hammer Horror.
16 - Humphrey Bogart.
17 - As Time Goes By, Casablanca.
18 - Ride Of The Valkyries, Wagner.
19 - Mozart.
20 - Superman, Supergirl, DC Comics.
21 - The Rolling Stones, lips logo.
22 - Doctor Jeykll and Mr. Hyde, Robert Louis Stevenson.
23 - Uncut music magazine.
24 - The Brothers Grimm.
25 - Gary Oldman, Bram Stoker's Dracula.
26 - The words of Vincent Van Gogh.

BOOK REVIEWS

RICHARDVALANGA
THE SUNDERLAND VAMPIRE

Late at night, a man awakes in a Sunderland cemetery and is confused and alone. The man cannot remember what has happened and has no recollection of the events that have led him to such a cold and desolate place. Why was he there and more importantly... who was he?

It is not just his loss of memory that is worrying him though, it is the strange new urges that are calling to him from the surrounding darkness, unnatural thoughts that seem somehow familiar... and disturbing.

The Sunderland Vampire is a psychological paranormal mystery thriller and a ghostly gothic romance that ultimately leads back to the coastal town of Whitby.

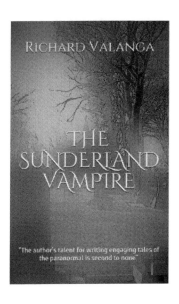

'It oozes Anne Rice...'

'A great book! Loved it.'

'This is brilliant, wonderfully vivid, very detailed and sumptuous and a pleasure to read.'

'Thrilling and intriguing, I love this book!'

'Great writing... great work!'

<u>'Don't put this down - someone will steal it'</u>
'This handbag size novel **is a total treat to own**. I read it in one sitting then my daughter who has similar tastes as I do started reading it. **From the beginning it draws you in** and you will delight at music references throughout, Sea Breezes by Roxy Music a favourite. **My only request to the author is to write some more!'**

Engaging and haunting...
"The Sunderland Vampire" - Late at night, a man awakes in a Sunderland cemetery and is confused and alone. The man cannot remember what has happened and has no recollection of the events that have led him to such a cold and desolate place. Why was he there and more importantly... who was he? It is not just his loss of memory that is worrying him though, it is

the strange new urges that are calling to him from the surrounding darkness, unnatural thoughts that seem somehow familiar... and disturbing…. -

I've never not enjoyed a novel by Sunderland born author Richard Valanga. **He never fails to deliver on giving the reader a truly ghostly paranormal experience with his supernatural writing talents. His flair with words is exceptional** and this psychological paranormal mystery thriller with a ghostly gothic romance leaps off the page with an engaging and haunting ambience.

A novella that packs a punch, "The Sunderland Vampire" is a perfect Halloween read (or for anytime of the year around a roaring fire late at night) and is suitable for readers of all ages.
#TheSunderlandVampire - 5 stars
Miriam Smith.

RICHARDVALANGA
THE WRONG REALITY

Running to save the life of his son, Ryan Walker and the Reverend Daniel McGovern are transported to another reality by an enigmatic blue ripple that suddenly appears on the Tyne Bridge.

For Walker, this reality provides everything he has ever desired except for the complications caused by the death of his ex-wife.

For the Reverend, the other reality is absolute Hell, a Hell that is tearing his vulnerable soul apart.

Murder, blackmail, dark eroticism and a dangerous religion threaten the sanity of the two men but there is a way back to their own reality, a possible window of opportunity that could enable them to return...

The problem is; will they realise this in time as both men are slowly being consumed by their alternate personalities.

'The author's talent for writing engaging tales of the paranormal is second to none.'

'The Wrong Reality for the real world...'
'Richard Valanga's **talented and imaginative** writing style is so suited to the supernatural genre and this together with a mix of horror and dark eroticism, **"The Wrong Reality" is proof of his superb eclectic ability to engage his readers in a truly alternative world.'**

'Excellent read; nostalgia, horror and mystery.'
'The whole theory of one's world being turned on its head is both fascinating and terrifying. **Richard has hit the mark once again**.'

'SUPERnatural - Another **thought provoking** novel from this North Eastern writer.'

'Not like run of the mill sci fi - Haven't read a lot of science fiction but this had a believable storyline, plausible characters, **couldn't put it down until I'd reached the end.'**

'A book to entertain and challenge you.'
An excellent read! An interesting book ... it stays with you after you put it down. It starts like a British version of **Sartre's Roads to Freedom trilogy,** but veers off into something else a third of the way through, yet retains the existential thread. **A truly amazing book.**
A well constructed book in all ways. **I highly recommend it**, if you want a fantasy, sci-fi story that challenges you & asks deep questions. Lovely easy to read style, **he leads you deeper into the recesses of you mind than you planned to go.**

'Thought provoking and literally made me shudder in parts...'

RICHARD VALANGA
COLOSSEUM

In the theatre of death only evil reigns supreme.
During the Festival of Death in Rome, four American art students go missing. One of the students is eventually found dead, horribly mutilated as if by wild beasts inside the Colosseum.

One year later, Nick Thorn is sent by the New Sanctuary to help the father of one of the missing students, a desperate man who is still looking for his daughter.

The New Sanctuary believes that Thorn has a psychic ability, a 'special gift' that could help him; Thorn however has always denied such a thing, claiming it to be pure nonsense and probably the product of an overactive imagination instigated by his drinking problem.

Shortly after Thorn arrives in Rome, the Festival of Death begins again and another of the missing students is gruesomely murdered. It is now a race against time to find the other two.

Can Thorn find and save the remaining two students or will Mania the Roman Goddess of Death succeed in devouring their souls and satisfy the blood lust of her followers?

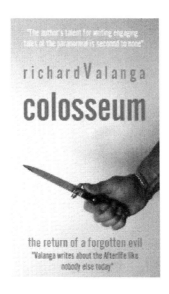

Another five star novel from Sunderland born writer…

Whenever you pick up Sunderland born Richard Valanga's novels, you just know it's going to be **filled with his most vivid imaginations and his incredibly engaging storylines,** for which he has put his heart and soul into writing them.

His latest publication "Colosseum" is no exception, this time with a visit to the chilling and haunting atmospheric location of Rome.

"In the theatre of death only evil reigns supreme. During the Festival of Death in Rome, four American art students go missing. One of the students is eventually found dead, horribly mutilated as if by wild beasts inside the Colosseum. One year later, Nick Thorn is sent by the New Sanctuary to help the father of one of the missing students, a desperate man who is still looking for his daughter. The New Sanctuary believes that Thorn has a psychic ability, a 'special gift' that could help him. However, shortly after Thorn arrives in Rome, the Festival of Death begins again and another of the missing students is gruesomely murdered. It is now a race against time to find the other two. Can Thorn find and save the remaining two students or will Mania the Roman Goddess of Death succeed in devouring their souls and satisfy the blood lust of her followers?"

This story is quite blood thirsty, as you'd expect from the ancient gladiator days. The author has included some really spectacular graphic scenes during the Festival of Death, that really set the scene for the plot. I particularly liked the first person narrative from Nick, I found him a curious protagonist, hard drinking, heavy smoking, Robert Mitchum lookalike with a sardonic humour and a similarity to the detective Philip Marlowe and his fellow American dime heroes. His special ability with his physic dreamlike visions make him quite remarkable and the perfect detective to help find the missing students.

There is no denying Richard Valanga's talent for paranormal and horror thriller writing. His visions just keep getting stronger and stronger. "Colosseum" is his most commercial outing to date following on from some very personal and emotive novels and he's a writer I'm more than happy to continue to follow, in the future.

Excellent gripping novel   - Amazon Review 26/11/2020

Great thriller!

When a number of students go missing in Rome and one of them is later found dead in the Colosseum, a man with supposed psychic abilities is sent to investigate what happened to the missing students.

He arrives just before the Festival of Death and when another of the missing students is discovered dead in a grisly manner, tension mounts. The race is on to find and rescue the other two students, assuming they're still alive. Were they kidnapped and killed by a secret Roman cult, and tortured by a sinister group of evildoers?
This is an excellent international thriller. Gripping and suspenseful. Highly recommended!

Stephen King meets James Herbert? Or Edgar Allen Poe.
Wow! What a story! Stephen King meets James Herbert! Maybe! A psychological tale with enough gore and horror to scare the living daylights out of you, yet **a plot to tease and intrigue you**, and characters you grow to really care about! **Well written, and excellently plotted**, this book cruises along at breakneck speed. Easy to read, very difficult to put down. **Highly recommended for those wanting a gripping, exciting story that stays with you**. This book needs a follow up …

RICHARDVALANGA
COMPLEX HEAVEN

Set in the North East of England, Complex Heaven is a psychological supernatural thriller that tells the story of a troubled soul tormented by the anguish of his distraught son. Called back from the Afterlife, father of two Richard; is concerned about the mental welfare of his youngest son JJ. There is a suspicion that somehow JJ is connected to the death of a young girl called Rose in Washington. The mystery however, is much more complicated as Richard finally confronts the evil that has been preying on his family for generations. A suffering that forces Richard back to the world of the living; where the answers to some of the darkest moments of his life are waiting.

'Complex and gripping.'
'I read this book in two sittings, very difficult to put it down. The characters are well developed and the plot twists and turns as it snakes to a dramatic conclusion. I heard through the grapevine that there is a sequel coming soon, it can't be too soon for me.' - **Mick Averre.**

'Brilliant, creepy and compelling!'
'I really enjoyed this **brilliant**, psychological supernatural book. **Totally unique** and wholly original I can't recommend this book enough!'

'Emotional rollercoaster I want to ride again!'
'When I started reading this book it brought forward so many emotions I had kept locked away. **It captured me right from the start and I couldn't put it down until I had finished!!** I would definitely recommend it.'

'Gripping'
'I started reading the sample to this book and could not tear myself away. I love the style, subject and setting. I have received my own copy of the book this morning and cannot wait to continue reading.'

'A resonating read for fans of the paranormal. Excellent!
'Profoundly thought-provoking and so descriptive at times I found myself there! An intense journey - but an enjoyable one. Would highly recommend.'

'A gripping read.' Complex Heaven is **imaginative and original in style and content. Definitely a must read.'**

RICHARD VALANGA
COMPLEX HELL

'It's present-day Sunderland and a mysterious manuscript is discovered in the house of an evil spirit, leading the unwary reader to a tale of the sixties in North East England, where not everything is quite as it seems. Forbidden love, loss and a lifetime of pure evil lie in store for whoever dares turn the ageing pages further. In Devils Wood House the memory of the missing girl, Rose, waits desperately. Unfortunately for her, time is not on her side. Can her soul be saved or will the child be lost forever?'

"Richard Valanga writes about the Afterlife like nobody else today, he's the 21st-century Dante of the North." - Tony Barrell, The Sunday Times

'Unique and interesting, thought-provoking, original and creative, it certainly is a tale that will stay in my mind.'

'Creepy paranormal read.'
'The author has a **wonderful and unique writing style** that draws you in instantly. "Complex Hell" is a wholly original take on the afterlife and quite believable too.'

'The author Richard Valanga writes like a poet and has a brilliant and impressive imagination to match.'

'**A good read, good memories and pretty good musical taste...**
Once again Richard **Valanga excels in not only scaring the reader to
death, but evokes fond memories of a time when things were simpler**,
when mobile phones and computers were still in the imagination of
Science Fiction writers! I feel sure Mr Valanga actually uses the
typewriter mentioned in the first chapter! A good read; good memories
and pretty good musical taste for something undead. **Richard writes like
a man possessed**...because I think he probably is!'

'**A very good read.**'
'This book was **a very good read, great concept**. Scary, but engaging; **I
was compelled to keep reading.**'

RICHARDVALANGA
COMPLEX SHADOWS

Fleeing Devils Wood House in Washington with a car full of ill-gotten
riches; a father and his son check into the Seaburn Hotel on the
Sunderland coast.

With them is the father's old manuscript which is his account of what he
experienced in the jungles of Burma during World War Two. Where there
is war there is immense evil, a breeding ground for dark supernatural
forces that once encountered will change your life forever.

This book is the third in the Complex Series and helps explain why one
family becomes entangled with and haunted by the malevolent Dark
Conscious.

'A great read!!'
'I really enjoyed reading this creepy, ghostly and at times scary book.
You could truly feel how passionate the author was about his personal
and emotional memories during the first half of the story. The whole
storyline comes together flawlessly at the end and was certainly quite
emotional. **Richard Valanga is a highly talented and imaginative
author and I highly recommend this wholly original book**.....it really
is a frightening thought that the dead do walk our streets!!'

'**Richard Valanga's amazing book Complex Shadows is not for the
weak- hearted.**'
'The past can be intense and in this supernatural and extremely dark
thriller that takes place in the north east of England (Sunderland to be
exact) he adds more to this 'one of a kind' read that will have you captive
from the start with great visions of the harshness and ugly events of
Burma during World War Two to the Shadows of the Past which most of
us can relate to.
    **The attention to detail in this fine piece of work sets this apart
from a lot of supernatural and paranormal books I have read.** If I
was a betting man and with an outstanding Hollywood agent, **I could see
this on the silver screen** with an outstanding soundtrack that will draw
you into this fabulous read.'

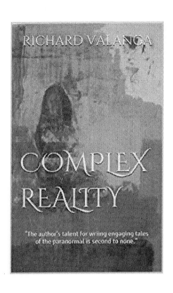

RICHARD VALANGA
COMPLEX REALITY

This is the story of one family's unfortunate entanglement with the malicious evil force known as the Dark Conscious.

A paranormal journey that takes you from present day Sunderland back to the sixties and then even further back to the World War Two jungles of Burma and the horrific beginnings of the story.

Can this persistent deadly evil be defeated, can the reborn spirits of a man and his father finally triumph over the darkness that threatens them and achieve everlasting peace for their family?

"Richard Valanga writes about the Afterlife like nobody else today, he's the 21st – century Dante of the North."
   - **Tony Barrell, The Sunday Times.**

A Great Read!
'A unique and intriguing supernatural tale that blends fact and fiction and leaves the reader questioning the eternal questions of life and death!'

"Fantastic, entertaining read."

"**Absolutely loved this book.** It hooks you in **from the start, triggers your imagination and keeps you entertained** with great references to north east locations throughout. **Definitely recommend this book to anyone who enjoys science fiction, horror or just an entertaining read.**"

RICHARD VALANGA
BLIND VISION

To see the evil dead is a curse...

It begins with the Roman exploratore Stasius Tenebris and the Calicem Tenebris (the Dark Chalice) - a vessel of evil that is brought back to life years later by Ethan Chance, a young man who was cruelly blinded by falling into an ancient Roman well when he was nine.

Was it an accident or did the spirits in the well choose Ethan for a reason? ...the Calicem Tenebris restores his sight but at a price.

This is the story of the chalice and the village called Darwell and the dark fate awaiting its inhabitants at the Festival of Healing.

Can Ethan, his friends and a knight from the Crusades save the day or is Darwell doomed to forever serve those who worship Mars, the Roman God of War.

'Blindingly good book'
This is the second book by Richard Valanga I have read and it's even better than his first, Complex Heaven. **If, like me, you enjoy fantasy novels that you can't put down then this author is for you.**
- Mick Averre.

'Brilliant!'
'Although "Blind Vision" is primarily aimed at young adult readers I still thoroughly enjoyed this book, I was drawn into it from the very first page with **great characters and a truly intriguing dark supernatural story line.** Set in 2 time frames- present day and fantasy Roman/Crusaders the story comes together brilliantly in a very detailed and fascinating way.'

'Richard Valanga is a great writer who has a fantastic imagination and I would happily recommend "Blind Vision" to readers of any age - you won't be disappointed!'

'The end is very exciting. You can feel the tension in the air. You can't put the book down. You just want to read faster and faster to find out what's going to happen. It is absolutely amazing. **One of the best books I have ever read.**' – A Young Adult reader.

RICHARD VALANGA
THE LAST ANGEL

When the unbelievable finally happens, who will be the one who will save us all?

Heaven is no more. All the Angelic have gone and the world is about to be consumed by a Dark Conscious, pure evil as old as time itself.

After thousands of years of exile, one of the banished Angelic finally returns to Earth.

Is he the last angel? Or are their others like him who will join him in the fight against the inevitable darkness that threatens the world of the living.

First reactions…

"I have just started reading The Last Angel **and I am totally gripped!**"

"Cracking!"

THE MUSIC OF FAMILY AND ME
a memoir
RICHARD VALANGA

Family were an English underground progressive rock band of the late sixties and early seventies. Brilliant, eclectic, original and unique are just some of the words that describe Family, a band fronted by the amazing singer songwriter called Roger Chapman who still continues to excite people today with his excellent solo career, check out his latest brilliant album called Life In The Pond.

In this memoir, I use the music of Family as a vehicle to journey back in time as I review each album and each song to see what memories they open up for me. I really hope that you enjoy this personal trip which I primarily wrote for my son James. For me, Family were the best, they produced music like no other, it is as simple as that.

revisit, review, recall

"I have to say **I feel humbled** in a big headed sort of way. Anyway, tell Richard it's great to read 50/100 pages of great reviews & **I appreciate it very much.** If he could send me some copies when published, I'll circulate to the people who I think & hopefully himself count. Again thanx very much, **a real honour**. Cheers, **Roger Chapman**."

"Cheers & must say **love the idea** as it also brings me back long forgotten memories good & bad. - **Roger Chapman**."

Wow!!! I am now starting the chapter about Family's 2nd LP, "Entertainment." What is so nice to read is the author's memories juxtapositioned next to his discussion of the music and the times in his life and world make this **such a warm, inviting reading experience**. This combination engages me on diferent levels. Even better, Richard Valanga's book causes me to reach for the CD'S that he is focussing on. Music is a universal language. So is the lexiconic message in words**. This gentleman does this exquisitely!!**
I would most highly recommend this book. Especially, if you loved the band Family and the music of Roger Chapman. (By the way, Roger's new CD, at 79 years young, **"Life in the Pond"** is also an incredible slick of **fabulous Music of the highest order**.)
David Freshman.

What a great book to read about the songs of **Family**, the British band. This band operated on so many different musical levels and styles! **Richard Valanga's work is so unique in that it juxtapositions his life and how the songs and music of Family made him feel.** This book is a fast read with **great insights** and defining understandings of the inner workings of the band and their music.
With **great details** explained by Mr. **Roger Chapman**, the lead singer/lyricist in the iconic band, the veracity and meanings become all the more **focussed and clear.**
A great book to have! Great work Mr. Valanga!
David Freshman.

I've had the privilege to read this before it went to print, and I have to say that **I am mightily impressed by this tome, to the extent that I couldn't put it down!**
This book is different from so many other Rock biographies in so much that it connects Valanga the writer to whatever he was doing at the time, and it does this in a song by song album way. So not only do you get a history of the writer as he came of age he carefully juxtaposes his life with the music of Family as it came out of the gramophone round a friend's house, or the radio at work, or in concert in Sunderland - **quite clever really...**
Simon Boxall.

Great Book
It was about time someone wrote a book about Family! Along with the Beatles and Led Zeppelin they were one of the most influential in my career as a musician. It gives **a great insight into the band and it's music. Fantastic writing** from someone who undoubtably loved Family as much (if not more) as I do.
It's a must have for me!
Paul Thompson - Roxy Music.

A mixture of 'High Fidelity' and '31 Songs' THE MUSIC OF FAMILY AND ME is **a very readable tale of fandom, obsession and heartache.** It is a great example of what music means, not only for teenagers but to people of any age!
Marc Andelane.

A great read
Love this book. As a lifetime fan of Family it's great to relate back to the memories of the group and the legacy of the music. Richard used his memories of the group to paint a .picture of the albums and the live gigs I could easily relate to. **A lovely nostalgic trip back.**
Tony Upton.

Entertainment
Excellent read chronological review of the great band FAMILY. **Well done Richard** got me to play all the albums again. **Thank you.**
Eddy.

Excellent!
I **really enjoyed reading this book** and reminiscing about my favourite band and their songs.
Mr Paul D Barnett.

Great Family read
Richard **takes us through every album** release and I'm right there with him.
David Jeanes.

A **fantastic** read from one of the finest rock bands Britain produced.
John Atkinson.

Evocative Memoir of a Great Band
Never saw Family perform live since I was a USA midwestern boy/man. But **this personal memoir helps evoke what being there in the UK in those heady days would have felt like.**
Richard L Giovanoni.

A criminally neglected band from the 70s gets it due - 5 STARS
In the early 70s a friend from my high school years Mike Green came back from a hitch-hiking trip he made through England. As was common back in the day Mike and I talked music when we got together, specifically we talked about the music scene in England this time. Mike knew I loved the bands Yes and Jethro Tull, " Yeah, Yes and Tull are big in England like here in the States", he mentioned. He went on, "But you know what? There is a different scene going on in England than here." A band called the Move is big "over there" he told me and there is this other group that is bigger than all of these... Mike loans me a record by this band that goes by the name Family, the record is FEARLESS. I notice the album has this multi-leaf cover, that is pretty novel, and I take it home and put it on with no expectations (the best way there is to listen to a new record if you ask me) and no previous knowledge of the band. Putting side 2 on first (a habit of mine) Take Your Partners spills into my room from my console tv/ record player combo I had at the time. There is this squiggly, funky electronic intro first, then the percussion starts slowly kicking in and with the first minute of Take Your Partners my consciousness takes immediately to "something" in this music, others have called the experience the sound of surprise (always a good thing to adventurous listeners). It was playful, syncopated and very English in a way I had yet experienced at the time.

So it went over the years with each of their albums. Each one with a different vibe that drew me in in some way as Take Your Partners and the rest of FEARLESS had. I played Family to friends who came by my place, but I can't recall anyone being all that impressed with them back in the day. Undaunted and in some way emboldened it made their music more endearing to me, they became one of "my" bands.

Fast forward to almost 50 years later I come across the Facebook group Richard Valanga leads - **Family With Roger Chapman Appreciation Society. There I found the music I love by Family**, the solo music of Roger Chapman and other members of the band cast in a new light. **Here were droves of mostly folks from the British Isles who took for granted all along that Family was the greatest band ever.** I was like Dorothy landing in Oz. I love the insights into a favorite band of mine from fans who were boots on the ground back in the day. So many stories from the past as well as current heads ups to recent developments with the band and members. Not the least of which came from the current book's author Richard Valanga.

With this as a lead in I was all set for Richard's book THE MUSIC OF FAMILY AND ME. **This is not Richard's first book and clearly is a labour of love.** The hours I shared with friends like Mike Green at the beginning of this review, hours talking about music come back in rich ways as **Richard shares his love for the music of Family. This was unexpectedly and especially endearing about this memoir.** Check it out. Doesn't matter if you are a die-hard fan or a complete and total novice like I was in 1972. Read the book and re-hear the music in tandem; or hear the music fresh to your ears and go the book for a clear perspective that Richard lends. **Either way this book is a winner.**
Jeff Gifford.

RICHARD VALANGA
THE NEXT REALITY

To get to Heaven
You have to go through Hell

The Blue Ripple is an anomaly of nature that will transfer your mind to another reality.

A young man risks the Ripple to see the woman he had loved and had died in his reality.

The man is accidentally joined by investigator Nick Thorn in a strange twist of fate that makes them battle the dangers of a different world together.

Murder, abduction and dark eroticism await the two men in the deadly and vicious next reality.

Will love prevail?

Or was the journey a leap of faith too far?

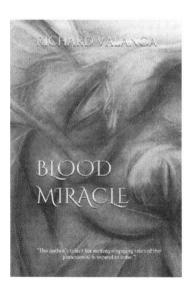

RICHARD VALANGA
BLOOD MIRACLE

A theological mystery thriller.
A young man with amnesia finds himself in an isolated farmhouse during an unnatural heavy snowstorm. Where is he, who is he? Mysterious dreams, sudden hallucinations, enigmatic artworks, contemporary music, strange marble statues, compelling intriguing books, famous artists and an obsessive author become part of the metaphysical puzzle that builds in intensity day by day, threatening the young man's sanity as the answer to the mystery of who he is becomes increasingly crucial. Will Churchyard Farm experience a miracle; can the stranded, lost young man's sanity and his fragile soul be saved?

RICHARD VALANGA
DAY OF THE ROMAN

They all thought that the story of the Festival of Healing had been concluded.

But the shadow of evil is back in the northern town of Darwell, determined to find the Sword of Pluto, a sword that could determine the future of the world.

Ethan Chance is blind and has gone missing and his family and friends are worried. Ethan has a 'Blind Vision' that is capable of seeing pure evil and the living dead but now this power has mutated.

Where is Ethan and what is is his connection to the Sword of Pluto and the Shield of Saturn?

Can Ethan's friend, Adam Sunderland and an old Viking spirit called Ragnar save Darwell once again from the threatening forces of the ancient Roman AGOTE, who want to send the world back in time?

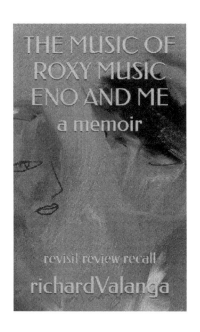

RICHARDVALANGA
THE MUSIC OF ROXY MUSIC ENO AND ME
a memoir

Inspired by the critical success of my Music of Family memoir, I decided to continue with a Roxy Music Eno memoir which sort of made sense to my personal time-line, the inclusion of my formative art college years.

So I drifted back to those golden years aided by the incredible music of Roxy Music and Brian Eno which was a vehicle to re-ignite my memories, a key to unlock those dormant thoughts...

We cannot go back but we can remember, the what ifs, the if only's, the heartache and joys of a young life and I always needed something to get me through the dark times and music was that something, a shining light of hope that has never faded.

Once again, this memoir is for my son James, a little insight into the life of his father when he was a young man so any unfavourable critical response to this book will mean absolutely nothing to me, all I can hope is that you do enjoy this memoir and I am sure that the music of Roxy Music and Eno will bring back memorable moments for you too.

Viva Roxy, viva Eno!

"Thanks for the memories!"

"I picked up the Sunderland vampire's latest edition of him. Devoured it in two sittings and thoroughly enjoyed it. I was more interested in Richard's life than the Roxy/Eno bits, although I was obviously into those too. I figure there's a couple of years between us and NE common ground, so a lot of it felt really familiar - from the plastic Beatles wig to the strangeness of leaving hyem for college. Thank you for sharing your memories and helping me relive mine. X"

"If you were present at the time, a great read, and even if you weren't!"

"Brought back so many memories of an amazing time in the music world. If you're a Roxy Music fan this is a must have. I lived in London at the time but can relate to so much of what Richard writes about.
Great stuff and also fascinating insight to the authors life."

"Another rapid page turner from the 21st century master of thrillers/nostalgia."

"I loved the reviews of songs, and memories of the writers younger days, it made me think I'd been there although I'm a bit younger and located miles away."

Printed in Great Britain
by Amazon